THE WIFE HE ADORED

A Clearwater Romance - Book Two

MEGAN MCCOY

Published by Blushing Books
An Imprint of
ABCD Graphics and Design, Inc.
A Virginia Corporation
977 Seminole Trail #233
Charlottesville, VA 22901

Megan McCoy
The Wife He Adored

eBook ISBN: 978-1-64563-945-9
Print ISBN: 978-1-64563-946-6
v1

Chapter 1

L ucy Arndt held her chihuahua, Juliet, close as she watched her best friend, Ellie, make her first speech as city manager. Ellie had been working toward getting that appointment, but not for two years when the current term expired, but the city manager before her had suddenly resigned, citing family and health reasons. Ellie had been pushed through by Mayor Shelia Lloyd and there were basically no dissenting votes from the council, who were probably relieved not to have to pay out thousands to do a search for a replacement. Who would have thought back in the day when Ellie was the only friend she had in the world, and she thought their lives would always run along the same path, that Ellie's life would turn out like this?

Ellie had a fantastic husband, and a brand-new house where she was attending a housewarming celebration tonight. Lucy had watched the house go up, but hadn't seen it at all the last month or so. Ellie wanted to surprise her with the final results. Now Ellie had a fancy new job and Lucy knew it was only the first step on her way up in the world. There would be no stopping Ellie, she knew. Her husband Mike seemed to support her in everything she wanted to do. Ellie was a lucky woman.

Flicking the TV off, she sighed and looked around her little house she had bought almost five years ago now. She loved her little house and adored Juliet. She'd had her about six months, since she'd found a new job and dumped – or didn't dump – Max Sutherland. She'd grown to love his little dog, Gypsy, and well, she thought she loved Max too, till she found out that she was only a fling. An afterthought. No one to be considered unless he was in The Mood. Then he'd be calling. He never took her on a real date, and never seemed to care about her, unless he was in bed with her.

She'd had a hard start in life. One of eleven kids, now twelve, she'd heard, she was number six, and mostly forgotten. She wasn't an older sister mom and she wasn't a younger with an assigned sibling to care for them. On her own mostly, she floated through her life, trying to never cause anyone any trouble.

Her mom and Ellie's grandma went to church together and she and Ellie had become friends. Often she was either at Ellie's house or Ellie's grandma's house and doubted her folks even realized. Her mom did what she called homeschooling which was basically assigning them all a number of work book pages to do each week. It had been a joke as she realized when she and Ellie compared homework when they were both in 9th grade. Lucy had been appalled at what all she didn't know, and worse yet, didn't realize what all there was to learn out there.

Ellie's grandma, a former teacher, had taken her under her wing and she had her GED and a spot in the same college as Ellie before Ellie graduated high school. Ellie's grandma always told her how smart she was and that she could do anything.

Her parents had not been happy. Her only choice in life

was to get married and have a large number of babies. Nothing more. That was fine if it was your choice, but it didn't seem to be a choice, but a rule. She had left home right before she turned seventeen, on very bad terms and still missed her mentor to this day. Ellie's grandma had passed away suddenly right before they both moved into the college dorm. She and Ellie both had lost an anchor and would always be closer because of their shared grief.

She loved college and kept changing her major so she could stay longer. She often worked two jobs while taking a full load and adored every second of it all. Managing to stay five years, Lucy ended up with a double major in business and accounting, and two minors in history and finance. College had been her first chance at a real life. She rarely got to see any of her siblings or heard anything from anyone but recently her younger sister, Moriah, had suddenly started slipping emails to her. Moriah was nineteen now and seemed to want help breaking free of the family and their restrictions. She would do anything for her, once she could figure out what to do, but right now, she had to get dressed for Ellie's party.

Getting dressed, Lucy felt the excitement rise. She did enjoy a party and this was at her best friend's house. She and her friend Jordyn were going to share an Uber out there, just in case they had too much fun. Ellie had said she could stay the night but she would Uber home. She didn't want to leave her little Juliet that long, after all. Kissing the top of her head, she gently put the little dog on her bed, then went to the closet. "What should I wear, baby girl?" she asked. This month, her naturally dirty blonde hair was a golden blonde with pink highlights. She picked out a dusty rose-pink dress that fell to just below her knees, and beige sandals. Loose enough to be comfortable and fitting enough to make her feel good. So nice to have choices other than the 'modest' wear she and her sisters had to choose from. While her clothes still now were mostly modest, they were in bright fun colors. She wore pants and jeans and even a tank top when the mood struck her. It felt so freeing, even if she felt pangs of guilt now and then. Half an hour later, she ran out the door with her purse and gift bag in her hand. She couldn't wait to see Ellie's new house.

"Hi, Jordyn," she said as she slid into the back seat next to her.

"Are you excited about the party?" her friend asked. "I had to take off work tonight to go to this thing."

"I am very excited," Lucy confessed. "I bet Ellie's house is fantastic and I can't wait to see how it looks."

"I heard Miranda did a great job on it," Jordyn said. "I'm looking forward to it, too."

"Was your client upset that you had to take tonight off?" Ellie asked.

Jordyn shook her head. "Nah, I gave them enough notice. They went to St Louis for the weekend and are probably eating better than they would be at home."

"I doubt that," Lucy said. "You are so good. I'm surprised Ellie didn't ask you to cater tonight."

"She did. I said no. I wanted to just go to a party and not work for a change," Jordyn sighed. "I so rarely get a night off, you know."

"I know," Lucy said. Jordyn was a private chef working for three families, cooking for them all two nights a week, but making them all three meals when she came over. One for that night and two to save for later. Then she occasionally catered parties like Ellie was throwing tonight and Lucy knew she really wanted to grow that part of her business. "I'm glad you get the night off."

"Me, too," Jordyn said. "I can't wait to get there."

"Won't be long," the driver said. "A couple more minutes."

Lucy looked at all the cars lining the big circular drive

Ellie had insisted on and was glad they didn't have to worry about parking or hiking in dress shoes. She had a big turn out tonight. Her breath shook a little as she got out the car door. Max could very well, okay, would be there. It looked like a big party. Hopefully, she could ignore him, but if not, then she would act as if he meant nothing.

He'd been her first. The first one to break through her upbringing and convince her that sex outside of marriage didn't doom you forever. Now she wasn't so sure he was right, because she felt doomed, as much as she faked being happy. She thought it meant they were involved. A couple. He thought it meant he could come and go as he pleased. No romance. Nothing but a good time. She wanted more than a good time. So he did not matter to her. It was as simple as that.

Ellie and Mike stood at the front door as they came in. "Lucy, I'm so glad you are here. Thank you for coming," Ellie said, then whispered, "That is my official greeting. But I'm really glad you are here. Go look around, tell me what you think and who Miranda is drinking with."

Lucy giggled. "Will do, I can't wait to see it and be your spy."

Jordyn, she noted, was already at the canapé bar, probably judging the offerings. She was caring for her elderly mother who lived here in town, and Lucy knew that otherwise, Jordyn would be off working in a big city, in some big fancy restaurant. The woman had real talent, and amazing knife skills. What she could do with baked goods rivaled any on the TV shows she sometimes watched.

Now, she would have to check out the house and do a little reconnaissance on Miranda, the woman who had designed most of it, and who was a thorn in her friend Ellie's side.

Gasping as she turned the corner into a big living room, she saw Max with Miranda. That was killing two birds with one stone, wasn't it? Deliberately, she turned the other way and went wandering through the house, suddenly wanting only to be at home with Juliet. She could leave as soon as she wanted, she reminded herself. She had broken free from the rules of 'should' and 'must'. But first she would check out the house. Because she wanted to and she could do anything she wanted to do.

One thing she really wanted to see was the double walk-in shower, and the other was the gazebo. Ellie had discovered Mike and Miranda having lunch together one day and the reason, she later found out, was he was making Ellie a gazebo with a koi pond beside it for a surprise Christmas present. Mike was nothing but perfect, wasn't he? Why couldn't she find a Mike? One day, probably, she assured herself. She had thought Max was a Mike but he was just a cad. Old fashioned as that sounded, it was what he was. A very handsome charismatic cad, but still.

She walked up the stairs to what she assumed was the bedroom area. After admiring the walk-in shower, she turned to go down to the gazebo before it got too dark outside. However Ellie met her halfway down the stairs. "Let's go up," she said.

"Sure," she said easily as she turned around. "I saw your speech. I'm so proud of you."

"Thanks for helping me write it," Ellie said. "I couldn't have been as eloquent without your help."

"Ahh, anything for my best friend," Lucy said as she followed Ellie into a small room, painted a lovely rainbow color. Like the hair she sometimes favored. "I love this room!" How had she missed it before? Too focused on the double walk-in shower, she guessed.

"Mike calls it the nursery, but I tell him that won't be for a while yet. However, I want to talk to you about something and tonight seemed like a good time."

6

"You can talk to me about anything anytime," Lucy said.

"Well, this is a special thing. I apparently have to have an administrative assistant in my new job and well, I only know one, but she is the best one in town so-" Ellie looked at her expectantly.

"Really, El? You want me to work for you?" Lucy didn't know what to think. Sure, they had worked on the speech together, but that was friendship only.

Ellie shook her head. "I want us to work together. If I run for mayor in two years I need you there with me. If I go beyond that, I need you there with me. This is just a start of us and our journey. We have both been seeking something for so long, and I think we might have found it. I'll send you over the job description tonight after the party and you can let me know soon."

Lucy didn't say anything, but hugged her close. The answer would be yes, but she'd be smart and look at the job description – and the salary – first. This sounded like a great opportunity though. Job hopping while fun and entertaining was getting old. She usually got bored with a job too quickly, and moved on to other challenges. Being very very good at her job made her easily adapt to any situation. This would be something new and different - city management would be rife with challenges. And if Ellie did go after the mayor's job in a few years, well, what was more challenging than politics? She did love a challenge.

"I have to go back to the party," Ellie said. "Talk soon. Love you, Lucy."

Overcome with emotion, Lucy took a minute, then smiled, went downstairs and headed to the back yard. There was a small, paved path to the gazebo lit by what she called fairy lights on both sides.

She headed down to it, thinking hard on what Ellie offered. It could be everything she wanted. She had loved helping Ellie write her speech. She loved being an admin. But, it was hard working for family and that is what she and Ellie were. Making that distinction between employee and family might be challenging. Losing her best friend and almost sister over a job was not an option. She'd lost too many people in her family when she broke away from home. Something to think about because she never wanted to lose Ellie from her life.

Everything seemed to be covered in those gorgeous twinkling fairy lights in the back yard and she picked her way down the path easily. This was such a great thing for Mike to do for Ellie. Halfway down, she froze. Two silhouettes were in the gazebo already. One she thought she knew, but the other she recognized immediately. Her gut knew that build, the shape of those shoulders, that silhouette, and her heart felt as if it were being cut in two. Lucy turned and ran back to the house, dialing Uber on the way. She had to get out of here. Right now. Looking around the crowded room, she didn't see Ellie or Mike to say goodbye and figured they would be busy anyway. Her heart pounded as she waited for her Uber, hoping no one would talk to her.

"Lucy!" No such luck.

"Hi, Joni, Hi, Beth, how are you?" Joni was Ellie's brother's next-door neighbor, and Beth was her reclusive sister. People rarely saw her, and often forgot she was around. She worked from home and seemed to hibernate there. Joni, however, was a bundle of energy. She taught middle school with a couple of her other friends, Shona and Izzy, and they all often went out together or got together. They had all been together for Ellie's bachelorette party. Who played Candy Land at a bachelorette party? This group.

Lucy relaxed a little. She'd be fine with Joni till her Uber came. "We are good," Joni said. "I finally persuaded Beth to come out of her hidey hole."

Max. Of course. Was he done kissing Miranda now? Her turn? Yeah. That didn't work for her. "Why were you hoping I was here?"

He moved her to the side of the hall out of the line of traffic. The party was getting busy. Ellie knew a lot of people, apparently.

"I've missed you." He smiled that easy Max smile and she frowned. She wasn't falling for that again. "How is the new job?"

Lucy felt startled, how did he know? Oh, he meant the one she was working now, not the one Ellie just offered her. Shrugging, she said, "It's fine. No one there thinks I'm a play toy to discard."

Max winced. "I guess I deserved that."

"Guess you do," she agreed. "I have to go now. My ride is here."

"Party is young," he started.

"Party is done," she said and yanked her arm out of his grasp. "Enjoy your life, Max." Walking away, she felt proud of herself. She handled that very well. And she could so wait till she was in the Uber to cry. Just watch me walk away, she hummed as she walked down the steps. That would show Mr. Max Sutherland she didn't care about him anymore. He could dump her and kiss someone else in the gazebo and she did not care. Not one little bit.

Lucy managed to slip out the front door without speaking to anyone and also managed not to cry till she got in the Uber. Tonight was just a win/win. She couldn't wait to get home to Juliet.

<hr />

Max frowned as he walked into work. Bryan was already there. He had just moved to town, following his spouse who was transferred to the hospital here in town. Apparently the spouse was a doctor of some kind, but they had yet to meet. They – he – had hired him after Lucy quit. He still didn't understand why she quit. They had a good time, and it was over. Why did women have to take everything so personally? Bryan seemed to like to show up early and stay late and do a good job, which wasn't bad, but Max was used to his early morning alone time in the office. But he liked Bryan. Not nearly as entertaining as Lucy, or as fun to flirt with, but still. The office ran smoothly, so there was that.

"Good morning, Max. Good morning, Gypsy," Bryan said as they walked in. "I have the coffee made and ready for you. The notes from your meeting last night are printed out and on your desk. Mike is already in his office."

"Thanks, Bryan," he said. "Let me know when Shelia Lloyd calls. And when she does, no interruptions, please."

"Will do," he said. Max missed Lucy and her sass and giggles and how her antics made Mike crazy. That was a fun part. Amusing and fun and once he broke down her barriers, great in bed. The fact she thought it was more than fun and games wasn't really his problem. Though it was because she didn't want to play with him anymore. Everyone liked him. He had never had a bad breakup, they always stayed friends. Until Lucy.

His face was the face of their company, though really Mike was the brains. Mike was the one making the good investments and better decisions, but he was the one who went out and made the connections and got the groups to invest with them. Mike didn't enjoy that as much. He was more of a one-on-one kind of person. He could hold a hand when the stock market went down, but he didn't enjoy the soliciting of new business. They were a good team. Right now, he was working with the mayor to get not only her personal business, but the town's investment business also. That would be a big coup to them. They had been working with the same company for years now, but with the city manager shake up, he thought now was a good time for a change, and just needed to convince them to go local.

He stuck his head in the office, "Hey, Mike you all recovered from the party Saturday night?"

Mike looked over from his computer, "Ellie was very pleased with the turn out. The bigger question is did you have a good time?"

Max walked in and shut the door. "Why is that the bigger question?"

"Well, according to my wife, who heard it from her best friend, someone was entertaining a certain lady in the brand-new gazebo I had built for me to have a good time in."

"What?" Max looked at his friend. He needed to speak plain English.

Mike sighed. "Lucy told Ellie she saw you making out with someone in the gazebo."

"What?" Max felt like a fool. He had other words at his disposal. He thought back and laughed. "Yeah. Miranda came out to the gazebo and apologized for what she did to me years ago. I told her she was fine, just behave, and gave her a hug." He shrugged. "But if people want to think I'm a game player and was having a good time, well, who am I to argue?"

"Our business reputation," Mike suggested. "We aren't in college anymore. What would the mayor think if she thought you were making out with randoms in public? That you were someone she wanted to invest her money with?"

"Kill joy," Max said as he went into his own office and sat down. Mike was right, though, he admitted. They had been a powerhouse in college, the two of them. Getting any girls they wanted. Playing at all the fun places. Mike had settled down though, after the Miranda debacle, and he, well, he really hadn't. Miranda looked like she had moved beyond it too.

She'd only been twenty, he reminded himself and took the break-up with Mike very badly, doing the stalker thing for almost a year after. When she couldn't find or get hold of Mike, she turned to him. For the most part, he thought it was amusing, because it wasn't him having to deal with it for real. But then he got tired of it, too, and shut her down. Not as effectively as Mike had, by turning her over his knee and blistering her butt till she promised to leave him alone forever.

Sure, he and Mike had scenes in the dungeons and at play parties, but he never thought about using any of the techniques in real life. Apparently Mike did. He'd worry about Ellie, but she was such a confident and seemingly happy wife, he really didn't think there was anything to worry about. It was always mutual fun at the parties. What he did to Miranda was not consensual. However, it had done what it needed to do, but Max had a little issue with the delivery, so to speak. It just bothered him that Mike didn't get consent for it. A little bondage and whipping between friends was one thing, but both people got something from it. All he'd done was punish and deter.

Mike tried to explain it like a traffic ticket. You don't consent to the ticket but you take it and mostly try not to do it again. Max wasn't sure he agreed with that.

His biggest problem right now, was what was wrong with Lucy? Why didn't she understand playtime? Why did she have to get feelings for him? Why did he keep thinking about her?

Sighing, Max turned on his computer and sat thinking about the little airhead blonde while waiting for his phone call from the mayor.

Lucy smiled as she looked in the mirror. Blue hair matched her mood perfectly today. "I love it, Tasha," she said.

"You always love it, Lucy," Tasha said. "But I do think blue looks good on you."

"You said that about the pink and green, too," Lucy said.

"Peacock was my favorite. Maybe next month again?"

"Maybe," Lucy giggled. "We'll see how I feel next month. See you then, and thank you."

Although blue had been her mood when she walked in the salon earlier, it really wasn't right now. She just felt better. She had given notice this morning on her old job and would be starting her new one as the City Manager's administrative assistant in a few weeks. It was going to be fun!

Then she walked out the salon door and saw Max leaning against his car and frowned. Why was he around? She'd had all she wanted from him at the party a while back. Maybe if she ignored him, he'd go away. Too bad she'd parked three blocks away and couldn't flounce to her car, get in and drive away. What did he want? She walked by him and once again, he grabbed her arm.

"What do you want, Max?" she almost spat out at him. "I'm not taking off my clothes for you in the middle of town square."

"That's disappointing," he said. "But actually, I'm here to apologize and buy you a forgiveness lunch."

She kept walking toward her car. "What are you apologizing for?"

"How about we sit down over some good food and I explain that to you?"

"I am not certain I'm in the mood for good food," she said, and kept walking.

"Well, I could buy you rotten food but you have to explain why you want that to the chef, okay?"

"Go away, Max," Lucy turned and looked at him. He was a handsome man, for sure. About six-feet tall, dark hair and brown eyes with flecks of green, muscled and lean and dressed in his go to work suit, he was simply easy on the eyes. And oh, the charm. He just exuded it. He knew all the right words to say and very literally, much to her chagrin, charmed her out of her pants. Well, she wouldn't make that mistake again. Fool me once, shame on you, fool me twice... he wasn't fooling her twice.

"Lucy, come on. I know you want to eat. I'll buy you sushi," he coaxed.

"And not make fun of me for being vegetarian?" she asked.

"You don't make fun of people on an apology tour," he said.

Well, she was hungry, and she did like sushi and they made fantastic brioche there and well... "No. What good would it do? You are sorry. I get that. I'm sorry I misunderstood everything. The end." She headed toward her car again. But she couldn't resist one more toss over her shoulder, "Bet Miranda wants sushi." And then finally, after what seemed like a million miles, arrived at her car. He hadn't followed her, she saw. Good. She didn't want him chasing her down the street. That is what she wanted. Him to leave her alone. And he was. Yay.

So why did she feel so let down?

"Mike?" She answered her phone, later that evening. "Is Ellie okay?" Why else would her best friend's husband, who didn't like her, be calling her? Something happened to her best friend.

"Yes, she's fine. Lucy, I need your help. I want to do a small little dinner get together for her birthday later this week. We just had this big party at the house, and really, how many parties does one house need in a week?"

"One is plenty," she agreed. "How can I help?"

"I was wondering, can you host a dinner for about eight or ten at your house as a surprise for her? I was thinking maybe getting Jordyn to cater? I'll pay for everything, including your time. I hate to ask you but…"

"Mike, I'd do anything for Ellie and I'd love to host a dinner. Ten people max, you think? That is no problem."

"Well, if Jordyn can cook we need to include her too, because we don't want her feeling left out. But I will let you know as soon as I get the RSVPs back. I just needed a spot and an excuse. She loves going to your house and would never expect you and I would be working together."

Lucy laughed. Mike had never admitted before she made him crazy. "True fact. I have room for that many. Are you going to talk to Jordyn and invite people or am I?"

"I'm going to do everything but host," he said. "All you need is room to seat us all. Maybe a pretty table decoration or something?"

"I can do all that! I'm so excited. Thank you for including me in this."

Mike sighed. "Basically you are my sister now, so I guess I need to get used to that idea, and you."

Lucy giggled, knowing Mike thought she was a total airhead and that she made him crazy. Ellie thought it was hysterically funny and often teased her, threatening to tell Mike about her IQ. Lucy had sworn her to secrecy though. It was a little fun to make cool, calm, collected Mike crazy after all. "Okay, sounds good. I'll try and tolerate you, too."

"Thanks, Lucy. I'll be in touch with details, time and menu and things. I'll let you know if Jordyn doesn't work out. Don't forget this is a surprise."

"I won't forget!" Lucy hung up. Okay, something to look forward to. She needed to clean her house and Pinterest birthday decor and, yay! Something to take her mind off Max, which she had worried about since giving notice on her job. She'd taken a few days between the end of one job and the beginning of her next one to do some job research and brush up on a few skills. So it would be fun to plan a little party.

For the first time in a while, she felt like her old self again. Lucy smiled and logged onto her computer to see what kind of decor she could do. Hitting her email, she saw a message from her sister Moriah. Sighing in anticipation, she opened it.

Hi, Lucy! Hope things are going well there. Nothing has changed here. Mom and Dad are still doubling down on the rules since you left. I'm writing this from the library computer, so don't know when I'll be able to check for an answer. Mom is here with the littles for story hour. They are still pressuring me to accept Ethan's proposal, but I'm not ready to get married and have a slew of kids like they all expect me to do. I know you have offered to let me come there, but I'm not ready to leave the siblings behind. Yet anyway. I just wanted to check in with you and let you know we are all good and miss you desperately. Love you. Moriah.

Lucy sighed and shut the computer. She'd have to answer her later. While she never regretted leaving the patriarchal lifestyle she grew up in, she did miss her siblings and hated she wasn't allowed contact with them. She did not miss all the rules, the no choices – a woman's place was in the home and nowhere else – the maxi skirts and the keeping sweet all the time. No one was allowed to show feelings if they were at all negative or uncomfortable, unless they were males. Boys will be boys after all. She was so grateful to have found Ellie and Ellie's grandma who helped her find her way into college and her own life. But still. Sometimes...

Resolutely she opened her computer again and logged on to find decor for Ellie's small intimate dinner party. This was going to be fun and she needed some fun!

Chapter 2

"Hey, Ellie," she walked into Ellie's small realtor office she was closing to take the city manager job. "Need some help?"

"I would love some. This is harder than I thought it would be," Ellie replied.

"Emotionally?" Lucy guessed.

"Yeah. I have worked for years to do this, but now, I guess my life is taking another direction."

"More than anyone else, I know how scary taking a new direction is," Lucy said, grabbing a box and taping it together so she could fill it with books.

"I realize that," Ellie said. "Have you heard from Moriah lately?"

"I got her weekly email sent from the library computer, but she didn't say much. Just they are still pressuring her to get married."

"She just turned 19," Ellie said. "That's sad. I wish we could help her."

"She knows we are here for her anytime, but she's not ready. It's scary, you know," Lucy said.

Lucy opened her arms as Ellie came over to hug her. "I can't know. I only know from the outside. You are the one who knows and I'm so proud of you for being so strong, smart, and brave."

Lucy looked around the room and whispered, "Shh, that's our secret. Most people think I'm an airhead and I like it like that."

Ellie laughed and Lucy went back to packing the box for her. "So, you and Mike doing anything for your birthday?"

Ellie shook her head. "We just had that big party last week and I'm tired. I don't want to do anything. I have a big new house, a big new job, and fantastic new husband. What on earth could I possibly need?"

"My lasagna?" Lucy said. "How about you two come over to my house for dinner that night? If you don't have a meeting. I know Mike doesn't like me much but maybe he can tolerate me for some decent food?"

"Maybe a chocolate cake?" Ellie asked.

"Sounds like a plan," Lucy said. "Talk to Mike and let me know for sure, okay?"

"Will do. You ready to start your new job?"

"I can't wait!" Lucy said and smiled, knowing she just got Ellie to her house for the surprise party. "We are going to rule that school! Well, city, you know what I mean."

They both giggled and quickly packed up the rest of the office. "You selling this place or what?"

"Renting," Ellie said. "I want to have a home base to come back to if this doesn't work out for some reason."

"That isn't a good way to go into the new job, thinking it won't work out," Lucy said. "Of course it will. You are going to be great!"

After helping Ellie load her car, she headed to the pet store to buy some toys and maybe a new sweater for Juliet. The weather was getting chillier and she didn't want her baby to get cold. Then she'd go home and make some food and eat while she worked on party plans. It was going to be so much fun. And then her new job would be starting Monday and life was going to be good. Despite Max. Without Max. She had no need of Max in her life. He was a wimp and a not very nice guy anyway. She was a strong woman, of course, which meant she needed a strong man. Being nice, kind, and thoughtful was just who she was, so she needed a man who was the same. Not someone who could use people and dump them without a thought. Where did someone find a man like her dream guy? She didn't know if they really even existed. Maybe Ellie's husband, Mike was as close as they came. Her brother, Hank, wasn't too bad either, but Lucy thought he and his neighbor, her friend, Joni were sort of a thing. She just wanted either to be alone, or to have a whirlwind romance like Mike and Ellie did. They met at Christmas time and fell in love dressed up like Mr. and Mrs. Clause. How could it get any more romantic? There was nothing wrong with wanting a little romance in your life.

The last thing she wanted was an iffy on again off again sort of sleezy affair where she felt like an afterthought. She had fought too hard to be an afterthought in anyone' s life. She deserved better and she knew it.

Parking her car, she ran into the pet store, hoping they had some new things for her little Juliet. Juliet was her little love, so sweet and snuggly, and she deserved the best.

As she walked in, though, heading to the clothing area, she heard a familiar yip and automatically smiled. Gypsy. Then stopped smiling as she realized what that meant. Max was there. The last thing she wanted was to see him. The second last thing she wanted was to turn around and run away like a little girl. Strong women did not do that. Taking a breath, she did what she did when she was nervous and slid into her ditzy blonde girl head. There was another lady looking at the dog clothes and she made small talk. "Look! Aren't they the sweetest things! I swear my baby has so many clothes, but she really needs a new sweater for fall. I was hoping they had them here!"

"They get new ones in every week," the lady told her. "I try to come the day they arrive to get the best. I have a little yorkie—oh, look! That one looks just like mine!"

And here came Gypsy and Max. The other lady started gushing all over Gypsy and Lucy felt a pang of jealousy. She wanted to love on Gypsy. Gypsy had been her baby, after all, for months, and she really missed her. Yes, Juliet was her baby now, but one didn't replace the other. Max was just cruel not allowing her to see Gypsy.

He and the other lady made small talk while she pretended to look at sweaters. Her heart hurt. She wanted to hold Gypsy. Yes, she missed the little dog, but not the big man.

"Hi, Lucy," he said as he moved closer to her. Lucy kept shoving hangers around as she looked at the sweaters and tried to decide if she wanted to answer him or not. The other woman grabbed two sweaters and left and she wished she had done the same.

"What?" she finally said. What did he want? What did he want her to say? Hadn't it all been said before?

"I need to ask you a favor," he said.

What?

"Umm, I don't think I owe you a favor," she said, pulling out a gorgeous autumn themed sweater that would look great on her little chihuahua.

"Well, it isn't really for me," he said, and abruptly handed her Gypsy.

"Hello, baby," she cooed, as she snuggled Gypsy to her, trying to fight back tears of happiness as the little dog licked her nose. "I missed you so much."

"She missed you, too," Max said. "In fact, she wants to

22

know if she can come spend the night next week? I have to be out of town overnight for work and she has to have meds every eight hours. I could board her at the vets, but, well, I'd just feel better if she was comfortable with you rather than locked in a cage all day."

"Of course she can," Lucy said, not even thinking. "I don't want her in a crate all day either. Oh, wait, what day? I'm off Friday through Tuesday. I start my new job Wednesday."

"Sunday night through Tuesday morning," he said. "I leave Sunday night and will be back really late Monday and could either pick her up then, or early on Tuesday."

"I'd love to watch her," Lucy smiled and kissed the top of Gypsy's head. "Juliet will be so happy to meet a new friend."

"Who is Juliet?" he asked.

"My new dog," she said, holding Gypsy in one arm and the sweater in the other. "The one I'm buying this sweater for."

"I didn't know you got a new dog," he said, and for some reason this seemed to bother him.

"There is no reason for you to know," she said. "You are no longer in my life." She kissed Gypsy and handed her back to Max, ignoring the tingle in her fingers and heart when their hands brushed. It meant nothing. Leftover feelings. Of course she had leftover feelings. She wasn't a cad or a player like he was. Is.

"Okay, thanks," he said. "I'll drop her off Sunday."

"I'll be home," she said. "For Gypsy."

Max watched her walk away, and smiled. Did she just subtly give him the finger? Sure felt like it, the woman needed kissed and kissed well, and then put over his knee and paddled properly. Then he sighed. What was wrong with him? He adored the woman. He just didn't want to get serious. Why not? That was what he'd been chasing around his brain for the last few weeks. Because he didn't want to, wasn't a good reason. Lucy was fun, and funny. Behind her airhead persona she was smart, even brilliant he'd discovered when she worked for them, though for some reason she tried to hide it. Her work ethic, despite her job hopping, was on spot. Impulsive, true, but that amused him. He still remembered her second week of work when she signed them up for the Christmas business decoration contest and hauled a six-foot tree into their office, without asking either him or Mike. It had made Mike nuts and made him laugh.

Was it because she annoyed Mike that made him keep her at arm's distance? He and Mike had been best friends since they were little. Mike's opinion meant a lot to him, of course. They were in business together, hung out together. But he was his own man, and didn't need Mike's approval for whom he did or didn't date. He shook his head as he moved Gypsy to his other arm. "Do you need a new sweater, too?" he asked her.

She didn't really answer but just snuggled closer. "Maybe another day." He wasn't in the mood to sweater shop. All he really wanted to do was follow Lucy home, spank some sense into her and then take her to bed. That wasn't an option, however.

He smiled again as he walked out the door. He'd see her twice more in the next few days though. She probably didn't know he was invited to Ellie's surprise birthday party.

"Hey, Jordyn, what's going on?" Lucy answered her phone.

"I was just setting a time to come over and start dinner prep for tonight," Jordyn said.

"Only thing I have to do is run out and pick up a few last-minute things, " Lucy said. "I'm leaving in about fifteen minutes and then will be home the rest of the day, doing a little decorating."

"Ellie is going to be so surprised," Jordyn said.

"I know," Lucy agreed. "I don't even know who all is coming. Mike took care of all that. You are cooking, and all I'm doing is the decorating. That's my kind of party."

"Well, you know I'm coming," Jordyn said. "Mike and Ellie. Probably her brother and maybe Joni. Not sure about who else. Max?"

Lucy felt a thrill of nerves. She hadn't considered that Max would be invited. Ellie knew what happened between her and Max, and wouldn't do that to her. But Ellie wasn't making the guest list, Mike was and he would more than likely invite his best friend. Well, that put a spin on things, but she'd think about that later.

"I just know there will be ten of us, Izzy and Shana are coming, " Lucy said. "I have the table set already, and some decor up."

"I'll let you get back to work," Jordyn said. "I'll be over in about an hour to start cooking."

"See you then. Park in the driveway and I'll help you carry stuff in and then we will move your car a little later." Lucy hung up the phone and slid it in her pocket. She'd arranged with a couple of neighbors to use their driveways for a few hours so Ellie wouldn't see the cars. She had the two bedrooms and the bathroom for everyone to hide in and then to jump out from and say 'surprise'.

"I'll be back, Juliet," she said to the little dog who didn't seem to care. She'd have fun with Gypsy next week. Juliet didn't get to play with friends often. Lucy had worried about exposing her before she had all her shots, though the vet had assured her it was okay, and now, well, they seemed to have as much fun on their walks around the neighborhood as they would in the dog park. Juliet was so little, and the dogs there were so big. And rowdy. But one on one time with Gypsy would be perfect. She'd hope they'd become best friends, but what good would that do?

Lucy ran her errand and came back home to finish her last-minute details and wait for Jordyn to show up. She needed to try and decide what to wear too. She was going to wear her jeans and light sweater but well… no. Max being there made no difference in what she was going to wear. She was going to be comfortable at the party she was hosting. It didn't matter who was coming. Or maybe she could wear that little red dress she'd gotten the other day and hadn't had a chance to wear yet. It needed to get out of the closet and have a little play time. It had nothing to do with Max. Not one single thing. Besides, it coordinated with the streaks in her blonde hair. Okay. Decision made. Little red dress it was.

Looking out her front window, she saw Jordyn drive up and went out to help her unload. "How's it going?" she asked as she went to the popped open trunk.

"I'm irritated," Jordyn said, looking a little frazzled. "I forgot the cake at the house! I was going to load it last, and then slammed the door, and left it. I'm going to start a couple things on your stove and then go back and get it."

"Want me to go?" Lucy asked.

Jordyn shook her head. "I know how to get it to the car without dropping it."

Lucy laughed, "And you don't trust me?"

"I do not," Jordyn said, "but I don't trust anyone else either, so there is that."

"That makes me feel better," Lucy said. "How can I help?"

"Just stay out of my way," Jordyn said. "I'm a one woman show."

"What are we having?" Lucy asked. "I need to know if I put the right place settings on the table."

"Lamb chops for those of us who indulge," she smiled at her. "But everything else you can eat. Spinach salad, garlic roasted potatoes, marinated white beans, asparagus, and my signature rolls with several flavored butters."

"My house has never seen anything so fancy," Lucy said, and Jordyn laughed.

"It's kinda like I do it for a living, isn't it?"

"Do you love it?" Lucy asked, watching her move pots and pans around.

"I really do," Jordyn said. "I love the science behind the cooking, the skills I've learned and especially seeing the look on people's faces when they eat."

Lucy nodded. She understood. She liked being good at what she did, but often wanted just a little something more, but hadn't figured out what it was yet. She had no real passion, except for learning, and her Juliet and well, yes, Gypsy too.

"Okay, I've got this started but nothing needs to be done till I get back. Don't touch anything! Will see you in a bit."

Lucy walked to her bedroom to change. It would be a little over an hour till people showed up. She got out her red dress and started taking off her clothes to change. She kicked off her shoes and pulled her jeans off, then heard a knock at the door. Jordyn, probably coming back for her keys or something.

"Come on in," she called and peeked out of her open bedroom door. Nope. That wasn't Jordyn.

"Did I get the time wrong?" he asked, his eyes raking her up and down. She hastily stepped back in the bedroom, pulling her dress over her head. She was fine. He meant nothing to her. She wasn't even surprised he was here. She'd expected him, of course. Him being here was a non-issue.

27

"Nope. Just in time to zip me up," she said trying to match his easy breezy no one cares tone.

"Yes, ma'am, I can do that," he said, coming into her bedroom. "You look great," he said, from behind, looking in the mirror while the zipper made an extremely slow upward trek. She shivered slightly and deliberately stepped away from him.

"Why are you here?"

"Because you needed help with your zipper," he said, not moving from the open door.

"Amusing," she said, turning away to change her earrings. Hopefully, her fingers weren't trembling too badly to put them in. Hopefully, Jordyn would show up soon.

"I actually came to spank some sense into you, but I think I'll wait till after the party."

"Doubly amusing. I am the one with the sense. You are the one who dumped me if you recall."

He looked mystified. "I didn't dump you, you left."

"After you said you wanted nothing serious with me. I'm not a play toy to be used and discarded." She managed to get her earrings in and turned around. "And what do you mean you were going to spank some sense into me?"

"Pretty clear statement," he said, still not moving out from the door. "I have never seen anyone more in need of a good spanking than you are."

"What has gotten into you?" she asked him and brushed by him. "Shut the bedroom door, please. You aren't acting like someone who only considers me disposable." She whirled around, and cocked her head at him and cooed, "Well, I do declare, Mr. Sutherland, it's almost like you decided you made a mistake and missed me." Lucy fanned herself dramatically. "I'd be so honored, if I didn't know it was a stupid lie to get my pants off again."

"Well, I was hoping to get your shirt off too at some

point," he said, "but first we will have to clear the air and I just don't think we have time to do it before the party starts."

Lucy laughed and rolled her eyes. "In your dreams, big boy."

"Don't dare a determined man," he said, quietly. "Jordyn is here and I brought Gypsy to meet Juliet." He motioned to the carrier in the corner.

"Go see if she needs help," Lucy said, trying to calm her breathing. What was wrong with him—what was wrong with her to react like that! He just wanted her back in his bed. He must have gotten bored and watched some of those movies everyone was talking about a couple years ago. She hadn't watched them, but knew there was a blindfold, some special room, a private helicopter and billions of dollars involved. Well, he had no private helicopter or billions that she knew about so that left him out, didn't it? She was no man's play toy. But she was the hostess for this party, so she put on her best golly-gee-everything's-fine smile and went to play the part.

"Well, hello, Gypsy. I'm glad you are here." Unlike the man who brought her. "Did you and Juliet meet? Why don't you two go to the laundry room for a bit while people are coming in? I don't want either of you to run out the door and get lost. Plus you can get better acquainted with your new sister." Now, why had she said that? They would never be sisters. Just friends. If that. Friendly acquaintances, probably.

Lucy looked around the room a bit later, after making sure the people had a drink as soon as they arrived. "Okay, I just got a text from Ellie. They will be here in less than fifteen minutes. There are the two bedrooms and a bathroom, hide in any of those. Ellie just walks right in my house, so we can all jump out and say 'happy birthday' when they come in."

"We can go ahead and put the appetizers out on the table," Jordyn said. "And pour the table wine. Then it should be time to hide."

"I'm so excited," Izzy said from the table where a few people had put gift bags and cards. "She won't be expecting this!"

"It was so nice of Mike to plan this," Joni said. "Nothing like a little romance in your life."

"I agree," Lucy said. "I adore how he takes care of her and loves her. Something every man should aspire to in a relationship."

"Absolutely," Joni agreed and punched Hank gently on the shoulder. "Step it up, boy."

Lucy smiled, well, that let that cat out of its proverbial bag now, didn't it? They'd all suspected Joni and Hank were more than friends. Now, they knew. Ellie would be thrilled. She wanted her brother to be happy.

"In the driveway! Everyone hide," Lucy said and she slipped into the bathroom and turned around to see Max had followed her in. Of course he had. He must have one thing on his mind, all right. Too bad for him. He shut the door behind them and looked at her as she heard the other two doors shut. Everyone must be hidden.

She didn't say a word. What was there to say? However he pulled her quickly into a hug and her traitorous body reacted to him, as it always had. Shutting her eyes as he leaned down for a kiss, she whimpered softly. "Not now, Max, please."

"Later then," he said, and let her go as she heard the other doors open and people yelling "Surprise!"

Quickly, she opened the door and stepped out, hoping she didn't look as flustered as she felt. Happily, in the chorus and exclamations of happiness and surprise, she wasn't really noticed for a few minutes. What did he mean by later?

"Lucy! I can't believe you kept this a secret!" Ellie said. "I thought we told each other everything!"

"Blame your husband," Lucy said. "This was all his idea. Jordyn cooked all the food and I just had the house."

"You are all wonderful," Ellie said. "Best birthday ever."

"Even better than our twenty-first at the casino in St. Louis?" Lucy teased.

"Well, okay, almost the best birthday ever," Ellie conceded as everyone laughed. "It was so wonderful of you all to do this for me, and this is lovely, a nice little intimate dinner with some of my favorite people in the world. Oh, and fantastic food, thank you, Jordyn." She raised her wine glass. "Cheers to you all!"

After the cake was eaten and the presents opened, people began to disperse. Jordyn started to clean the kitchen, but Max stopped her. "You cooked, I'll clean. I'll drop your pans and things off in the morning for you."

"Oh, you don't have to do that," she started, but he handed her the purse she carried in. "See you in the morning, Jordyn," he said firmly and Lucy saw Jordyn just shrug and smile. "Appreciate it, Max. Love you, Lucy. See you soon."

"You are so bossy, just like Hank," Lucy told him. Hank was Ellie's big brother and he had always thought he was the boss of them as they were growing up.

"Nah, I'm dominant," he smiled at her as he rolled up his sleeves.

"What's the difference?" she asked as she started to clear the dessert plates from the table.

"The difference is dominant is better," he said, filling the sink with hot soapy water.

Lucy laughed. "Well, that cleared that up."

"You are welcome." He grabbed a pan. "Lucy, I'm sorry I wasn't giving you what you needed."

"I have no clue what you are talking about," she said. He really wasn't doing this now, was he? Why? They were broken up, but had just gotten back to where they could see each other in public or with their mutual friends, without it being weird. Why did he want to make it weird again?

"Don't lie to me, young lady," he said. "That will earn you a trip over my lap."

"That is the second time today you've threatened to spank me. What's with that?" She was getting tired of this, and him. "I'm changing clothes and taking Lucy and Gypsy out for a walk while you, who volunteered to do it, clean the kitchen."

"Sounds good," he said. "Then we will have a little talk."

Lucy went to the bedroom, kicked off her heels and put on her sneakers. Then pulled her sexy red dress off, not wishing at all he was in there unzipping it, and put on her comfy walking the dogs' sweats, then took out her earrings and scrubbed the makeup off her face. He deserved nothing better. No reason to try and impress Max. What did they even have to discuss other than Gypsy's medicine next week?

She ignored him in the kitchen, snapped the leashes on the two dogs and headed out the front door.

"Why does he feel the need to suddenly talk?" she asked them as they walked. "I haven't changed my mind. I made a mistake, thinking he wanted the same thing I did, and when I found out differently we broke up. I don't see I did anything wrong, but believe him in the first place. Sorry, Gypsy, but your dad is a piece of work. He can turn on the charm like a light switch and make you believe anything, until I realized he only wanted one thing."

She watched the little yorkie and chihuahua do their thing and realized they were getting along really well for just meeting. That was a good sign, only because Gypsy would be here next week for a couple days. No other reason, she told herself.

Sighing, she finally decided that while she had no desire to go back home, she needed to. She and the dogs couldn't stay out here all night. Although it was a nice night. No. Home.

Reluctantly, she turned back to head to the house and whatever it was Max wanted to talk about.

Unsnapping the leashes as she walked in, she went into the

laundry room to hang them up and check the water bowl to make sure it was full. It was, so she had no other reason to stall, but headed back into the kitchen, reluctantly, with the two little dogs following her. He'd almost finished up, she noticed, and had Jordyn's pans washed, dried and put into the boxes she'd brought. He was handy in the kitchen, which was a good thing. While she enjoyed cooking, it wasn't something she did very often just for her. It was much more fun cooking for other people.

"Good job," she told him. "Did you bring Gypsy's medicine? I want you to show me how much to give her before you leave." That was subtle, she congratulated herself.

"I did, but I'm not going anywhere yet," he said, drying his hands on a towel and hanging it up. He'd wiped down counters and everything, she noted. He'd make someone a good wife. Then she chided herself for being sexist. What did he want?

"Here is the medicine," he said. "She gets three drops every eight hours. How many times a day is that?"

Lucy stared at him, baffled. "What?"

"How many times does eight go into twenty-four?"

"Is that a trick question?" What was he blathering about? "Three?"

"See how smart you are," he said. "First thing in the morning, mid-day and before bed, if you are getting eight hours of sleep every night like you should be."

Lucy rolled her eyes. How many hours she slept was certainly none of his business. He showed her the eyedropper, gave the little dog her medicine and then put both of them in the laundry room. "So we can have some privacy."

"Why do we need privacy?" she asked him. "I'm not getting in bed with you again."

"Well, how about a glass of wine and sitting on the couch with me so we can talk?" He smiled that charming Max smile

33

at her that made her melt. But she crossed her arms and sat at the end of the couch.

"I don't drink," she said.

What do you mean you don't drink? We all had wine with dinner? I've seen you drink a few times."

She shook her head. "No, you haven't."

"I sat right there."

Lucy sighed. "I don't make a big pronouncement out of it. I usually substitute juice or pretend to sip or order a virgin." Lucy blushed, but he didn't seem to notice her slip. "Most people really don't notice or care if I don't make a deal of it. Now. What do you want?" She did not intend to make this easy for him.

"I want to start over," he said.

"Start what over? Rolling in the sack? No, thank you. I've already gotten that t-shirt and have no desire for another one." This was not going to go well for him. "How dare you come in here and ask me to do that, knowing how I feel about it?"

"Honestly, if you'd told me you were a virgin, things would have gone differently," he said, sounding exasperated. Too bad for him.

"Yeah, defiling the good little girl was a big coup for you, huh?" She glared at him again. "You knew my background. You knew how I felt about things like that."

"It never once crossed my mind that you got all the way through college without having sex," he said. "Not one time, and that is really something you should tell a guy beforehand."

"Sorry." She managed to lay the sarcasm on as thickly as she could.

"Well, I owe you a good spanking for that, for one, and then for breaking up with me, for another."

"That makes no sense at all," she told him. "And if you recall, it was your fault we broke up, but really we were only together in my mind anyway." Spank her. What kind of utter nonsense was that? Men didn't hit women. Well, decent men didn't. Was he a decent man? At this point, she wasn't even really sure. Lucy knew she wasn't afraid of him, but would he really spank her? If so, why and if not, why was he continuing to talk about it?

"You have this big wall up," he said. "If we are going to continue to talk, it needs to come down."

"Why do I even want to talk to you?" Lucy said, and jumped up off the couch. "I feel you led me on. You lied to me either implicitly or on purpose because you are a jerk. I am hurt and feel like an idiot and really regret our time together."

"I am sorry for that," he said. "But not for what I'm about to do."

Lucy stared at him, confused, as he reached up, grabbed her arm and hauled her over his lap. "Now we can discuss things," he said, and smacked her bottom.

"What?" Her brain did not comprehend this. "Stop it, Max, what do you think you are doing!" It wasn't really a question as he smacked her again and she realized that talking about spanking her wasn't a euphemism. "Stop it! I mean it!"

"I mean it, too," he said and suddenly she realized her bottom hurt.

"Ow! Don't you dare!"

"I'm already daring and you've needed this for a while." He started smacking harder and faster and she tried to twist off his lap.

"Stop it! Now! Ow!" This was not getting her anywhere. She tossed her hand back to cover her bottom and he simply caught it and held it. How could he do this to her?

"Only way to get your attention and get through that stubbornness of yours."

"I'm not stubborn," she shrieked. "Stop it! Really! It hurts!"

"Spankings hurt," he said. And didn't stop. What could she say?

"I'll listen! Ow! Please!"

"Darn right you will listen." He didn't stop though.

"Please, please!" She felt like her bottom was on fire. What was he doing to her? Why? "Why?" she sobbed out. She would not cry. He couldn't make her cry. "No more!" He had to stop, she couldn't take this anymore.

She had never been spanked before and did not like it, one little bit. "It hurts! Stop it! Please!"

"Not quite yet," he said, as he continued to her ever-growing panic and dismay.

"No! I'm sorry!" she cried, not certain what she was sorry for. He was the one hurting her! "Don't! I'll be good." She finally sobbed in either frustration or pain, she was certain. But it had to stop!

Suddenly, Lucy realized she was on his lap instead of over it. All she wanted was for him to hold her and make things better and how stupid was that? She should be furious with him. But he was petting her, rubbing her back and saying something she couldn't quite understand as she tried to get herself under control.

"Why did you do that?" she finally managed to ask.

"You needed it," he said, pulling her into a tight hug. "We needed to clear the air."

"That didn't clear anything," she said, and sniffled. She needed a tissue.

"Sure it did," he said.

"Liar," she muttered.

"What did you say?" He tilted her chin up to look at him and she blinked the tears away.

"I said you were wrong. What got cleared? You don't know how I'm feeling right now." She sniffled again, feeling sorry for herself and a little bit of hurt feelings, embarrassed, and upset with him. But had no desire to get off his lap. She liked it there. No, she didn't. Yet, well, maybe she did. She noticed her bottom wasn't hurting very badly anymore. That was lucky for him! Why? She didn't know why.

"You are ready to listen to me," he said.

"Wanna bet?"

Max laughed a little. "Yeah, I'll take that bet."

"Good. I win. Pay up." She held out her hand and he took it, and kissed it.

"I'm sorry," he started.

"Good." She snatched her hand away, ignoring the feeling in her stomach. "You should be."

"Why?" he asked her, as if he really wanted to know.

"Because I was under the impression that you, well, that you and I were a thing. I didn't tell anyone that we were because it was so new, but I really, really thought so, and then I found out that you were just using me to play with," she said in one long breath. She'd been wanting to say that for such a long time. "And it really, really hurt. I'll get over it, but I'm not yet, and you spanked me and that hurt, too!"

He hugged her again, and she relaxed against him and sniffled. A tissue would be great right now. As if he read her mind, he reached over to the box and handed her two.

"Thank you," she said, blowing her nose and wiping her eyes.

"Okay, we need to start over," he said. "Taking you to bed was wrong, in a few ways."

"Because I sucked in bed?" she asked. She'd been wondering and felt mortified when he laughed. Instinctively, she buried her face in his shirt. Yeah, now he couldn't tell.

"Hardly," he said and kissed her forehead when she finally sat up again. She liked that. "We can talk about that another time, but right now, let's talk about starting over."

"What does starting over mean?" she asked him. How could they start over?

"How about a little romance?" he asked her.

"A little?" she asked, feeling suspicious. What did that mean?

"It means, will you go out to dinner with me when I get home from my meeting next week?"

"What are we doing?" Uncertainty filled her. What was he doing?

"You'll see. In the meantime, I'll see you Sunday morning with Gypsy. Thank you again for watching her for me, and thank you for the lovely party. You are a great hostess." With that, he leaned down and kissed her until she thought she'd melt in a puddle on the floor. Had he ever kissed her like that before? What was going on? He stood her up, finally, and she noticed her knees trembled. Why? She watched in silence, as he gathered Gypsy and the box of pans Jordyn left, and headed out the door.

What had just happened? Were they back together? What did a little romance mean and why wasn't she furious because he'd spanked her?

Chapter 3

"So are you and Lucy a thing?" Mike asked him as they sat across from each other in Mike's office.

Max put his feet on the desk and tilted his chair back. "Not sure yet. But I'm wanting to try again."

"Why and how did you talk her into that?"

"I took a page out of your book, macho man," Max said. "Put her over my knee, spanked her and then kissed her till she was silly."

"That wasn't a far trip," Mike said. For some reason Max didn't understand, Lucy irked Mike like no one else did. That amused him far more than he let on. Mike wasn't easy to fluster. "And she handled it?"

"Barely," Max said. "But she agreed to go on a date with me next week, so we will start from there and see what happens."

"I worry about your taste in women," Mike said, picking up the papers he'd been working on.

"So what else is new? Ellie excited about starting her new job?" Max asked.

"Seems to be. She closed her office, and has been studying

everything she can get her hands on, plus signed up for a couple classes on city management," Mike said. "And that's on top of everything else she does."

"The woman wears me out," Max said.

"Yeah, I'm about to wear out her butt if she doesn't cut back when this new job starts. No reason for her to be gone every night."

"She's always done that," Max reminded him.

Mike sighed. "Yeah, but now she has a husband who wants her home occasionally. I don't ask for much, but one weekend day every week, and a couple nights a week would be nice. I didn't marry her to watch her drive away all the time."

"Well, aren't you high maintenance," Max teased him. "Will that work, do you think?"

"What, blistering her butt? Only if I do it properly," Mike said. "Do you have everything you need to go Sunday?"

"I just came in to get those papers. Here's hoping we get this account," Max said. Taking the offered papers, he put them in the case he'd brought in with him. "Hopefully, I will get these signed before I come home."

"You better, and there better not be a lot of bar charges on your expense report."

"What? I have an expense account? No one ever tells me the good stuff."

Mike shook his head. "Ha ha. Call me if you need me and otherwise I'll see you Monday afternoon."

"I'll call from the airport before I get on the plane to come home," Max said. "You might want to give Lucy a call while I'm gone and make sure Gypsy is okay."

"Or you can," Mike said. "Tell Bryan I need those invoices done by the end of the day."

"I know when I'm being kicked out," Max stood up. "I'll see you Monday afternoon." But he would see Lucy when he dropped Gypsy off and again when he picked her up Monday morning. Then he was taking Lucy out to dinner Wednesday night to celebrate her first day at her next new job. That was what, the second one now since she quit on them a couple months ago? She had a nice house and didn't seem to be hurting for money, so he guessed job hopping didn't hurt her any. Still it was a sign of something. What, though? He'd have to find out. When they hired her, every one of her past jobs had given her excellent references, and he and Mike would too when and if called. She just didn't keep any of them longer than six or eight months, though.

What happened in that amount of time to sour her on a job so quickly? Why did she flit from one to another? They knew why she quit this one. Him. Bryan was good at what he did, but she had been better. It had seemed effortless, even though every time he or Mike walked in she put on her ditzy blonde act, and the office ran better than ever. Bryan was reaping the rewards of the new systems she'd put in place in the few short months she'd been there. Some he didn't realize she'd done until after she'd left.

He went back to his office and gathered the rest of the things he was taking with him. This was a big client he intended to sign. A vet who had franchised his office into several different cities, including Clearwater and that was where he'd heard they had lost their payroll accounting firm. He'd overheard the office staff complaining about their checks and did some research. If they could take over payroll, and with Bryan's input and help, they could, and then get their investment business as well, it would mean a huge influx of business and cash. He really wanted this. Mike loved dealing with the small potatoes, the individual accounts, helping people live out their best retirement years, but he loved the big guys. Together they made a good team.

Putting his laptop and his papers into his laptop carrying case, he frowned at something Lucy had said. Hell, he hadn't realized she was a virgin till after they were already in bed. He hoped he had handled her gently enough. She hadn't complained and had come back for more, so he assumed he did all right. He shook his head. The woman was gorgeous, smarter than she let people know, personable, a bit daft at times, which he thought was adorable, and yet... Yet, what? She was a conundrum and he enjoyed finding new things out about her all the time. He had missed her and selfishly, that wasn't fair to him. He worked hard and should get what he wanted, within reason. Plus she was a free babysitter for Gypsy while he was gone.

Frowning, he looked over at her bed in the corner. She wasn't in it. He walked into the front office. "Bryan, did you steal my dog again?" he asked.

"Well, it wasn't like you left her alone or anything," he said, swiveling his chair so he could see his dog cuddled on his lap. "Besides, she likes me."

Max shook his head and went back to his office after saying, "Mike wants to know if those invoices will be done by tonight."

"Already finished," Bryan said.

They had been very lucky to find him after Lucy quit. She'd stayed and trained him for two days and he hit the ground running. He'd just moved to town and bought a house from Ellie who knew he was job hunting. He'd followed his spouse to town, but Max hadn't met her yet. Ellie had recommended Bryan, knowing he was looking for a job. It was amazing how small Clearwater was sometimes. You could go seven steps to Kevin Bacon to about anyone you ran into around here. He liked that the town was big enough to have decent stores and shops and places to eat, and yet small enough, you often ran into someone you knew when you were out. Many people moved back here to start careers after college, like he and Mike and Ellie, others returned to retire here after working other places. Low crime, and decent established neighborhoods garnered it one of the Governor's Hometown awards a few years ago. Mayor Lydia was very proud of that fact.

Plus it was only two hours to Lambert St Louis airport, which made it handy when you had to go somewhere. He finished loading what he needed from the office to take with him and went back to the front office to collect his dog from Bryan.

"Do you have someone watching her while you are gone?" Bryan asked, handing the little dog over. "We'd be glad to, if you were planning to board her."

Max took her, and tucked her into his side. "Lucy is watching her for me. She has a dog too and they get along well, but thanks for the offer."

"Anytime," Bryan said. "Fly safe and I'll see you Monday. I'll be around and able to access the computer if you need me to look things up, or anything. Good luck!"

"Appreciate it," Max said, and left to go home, get packed, then drop Gypsy off with Lucy in the morning, and drive to St. Louis. It had been a while since he'd traveled anywhere and suddenly he wished Lucy was going with him. She would be so much fun on an adventure, he smiled. Her wide-eyed innocence and excitement at anything new. She just put herself into a situation with everything she had, with gusto as his dad would have said. But tonight he and Gypsy would be sleeping alone, without her. Shaking his head, he wondered why he had been so stubborn. Maybe it was true you didn't know what you had till it was gone. However, he had a second chance and he was going to romance his ditzy little blonde until she couldn't help but fall for him. Then what? He didn't have an end game in mind, but, well... He might have one, but he wasn't really ready to think about it yet. Other than putting that pretty little backside over his knee a few more times, before he had the pretty little blonde in his bed again, that he had vowed.

When he got to Lucy's house the next morning, he saw a note on the door. "Max, I ran out for a bit. Key under the mat. Leave Gypsy with Juliet in the laundry room and I'll be back in a few!'"

Max shook his head. One, he was disappointed he wouldn't get to see her, and two, did she seriously lock her door and then write a note announcing she was gone and where the key was? What was wrong with the girl? They would be having a discussion about that when he got back Monday morning. For someone as smart as she was, that had to be one of the dumbest things he'd ever seen. He ripped the note off, took the key, unlocked the door and went inside. As always, Lucy's colorful house made him smile. It was simply her. Nothing white, or muted, but bright and fun, from the carpet on the floor to the very bright blue couch covered in multi colored pillows, to the wild art on the walls, it was all Lucy. Fun, vibrant, and a little wild.

He put Gypsy and her bed in the laundry room with Juliet, and put the little dog's medicine on the counter, with a small bag of her prescription dog food. He double checked they had water and looked around one more time and smiled again. Then frowned as he remembered the note. The woman needed a keeper.

However, he left knowing that Gypsy would be getting great care while he was gone, there was no doubt about that. Had she left because she didn't want to see him today? It wouldn't surprise him if she was right around the corner, waiting for him to leave. Well, he'd be back early Monday morning for his dog and their discussion, but now, he had to head to the airport, so no snooping around corners for him. But she might find herself standing in a corner come Monday.

Lucy walked into the library with her hair piled up under her ball cap. Wearing that, big sunglasses, tight jeans, sneakers and an oversized jersey, she hoped she'd be unrecognizable. It was story hour for invited preschool and early elementary age kids, or that was the guise. It was actually a 'special' Sunday morning service that the library didn't sponsor but just rented a room for the people to use. Lucy suspected it was simply more brainwashing for the toddlers. Teach them young what the rules were, and put it under the umbrella of fun! They'd be more apt to learn and accept it, and bonus points, it was over by ten a.m. so they could be out of there, and on time for services.

It was also the one hour a week, Moriah managed to get on the library computers under the guise of research for school. Their mom was very lax on any schooling past about fourth grade and mostly left it up to the kids to scramble around and try to figure out how to learn. Preschool to third grade though, she took fairly seriously, and thus there were a couple toddler siblings attending story hour with her mom, which always included lessons and crafts. Julie, the sister younger than Moriah, had probably been left home with the new baby her mom had had after she'd moved out. She had never seen that baby but knew from Moriah's notes that it had been a boy. She was glad. Boys had it easier in their life. Moriah always came to the library though, to help wrangle toddlers till they got into the room, and because school. She was allowed to be alone because early on a Sunday morning there weren't many people in the library. Most people didn't even realize they were open that early.

Not that Moriah needed school, according to the parents. Girls were meant to fill the quiver, which basically meant marry early and have as many babies as they could to form an army for righteousness. How they were supposed to home-school a half a dozen or more kids with a substandard education themselves was a question no one seemed able to answer.

Lucy knew she loved kids but also knew she had raised as many as she wanted to raise for a while, she'd been a middle child and didn't even want to think about what her older siblings had to do when they were just children themselves. Maybe she wouldn't ever want any kids. Once the kids were weaned, their mother passed them off to the older ones while she attempted to fulfill the 'order' to have another arrow for the quiver. Ellie had teased her calling her a sister mom, but she'd never had a kid 'assigned' to her like her older siblings did and probably Moriah and Julie did now. She just flitted between them all when a sibling-parent needed a break or got overwhelmed or had other chores to do.

Yes, she missed her siblings desperately, but also hoped she was a beacon who let them know there were other ways to live. Her older siblings were all married and following in their parents' footsteps. If that made them happy, great, but really, how did they know it did unless they explored other options?

There she was. Lucy spotted her sister, sitting with her desk facing the room where the story time was held so she couldn't be caught doing anything horrible like emailing her wayward sister or applying to colleges like Lucy had done.

"Moriah," she whispered as she moved to the side of her. "It's me."

"Lucy?" she whispered back, not moving from the computer. "I'm so glad to see you!"

"Don't look," Lucy said, pulling out the computer chair opposite her. "Just let me know if you see Mom coming out the door so I can leave."

"I miss you," Moriah said, and Lucy saw her blink back tears.

"I miss you, all of you," Lucy said. "How are things going? How can I help?"

Moriah shook her head. "I don't think you can. Mama and Daddy are getting worse. They are so afraid of, well, I don't know what they are afraid of, but we are more locked down now than ever. This is literally the only hour a week I have alone. I wish I could get out of there, but I can't leave the little ones. They need me as a buffer."

Lucy felt racked with guilt, but still knew she couldn't go home. She just couldn't. "When you are ready to leave, I will help you. I have a second bedroom," she said. "I'll help you get into college, get a job. Get some comfortable clothes," she teased gently, blinking back tears.

"That will leave the work all on Julie, then," Moriah said. "I can't do that to her."

"You mean you can't do it to her till Daddy finds someone worthy enough for you to marry, then you will be out of there," Lucy said, despair filling her. "I love you. There is more to life than raising babies and submitting to authority all your life."

Moriah shook her head. "Ethan is pressuring me to marry him soon. Mom and Dad are making it quite clear that I need to – oh – I love you and I am so glad to see you, but the door just opened to the kids' room. Mom will be out in a minute. Don't let her see you with me, or I'll be in trouble."

"Take care. Contact me if you need anything, I'll try to come back next week," Lucy said as she got up and headed for the door before the first child burst through the door. She didn't look back but drove back to her house, hands shaking and heart pounding. Maybe Max hadn't been there yet and she could see him.

No. This was something he didn't need to know about. No one who hadn't lived it, would ever understand. Did she feel better or worse than before she saw her sister? They had been fairly close growing up, despite a brother between them.

At least she knew nothing horrific was going on. Right? Yeah. It was just the same old and Moriah knew she had her if she needed her, like she'd had Ellie and Ellie's grandma. She'd pay it forward if given the chance. It was scary to leave, she knew. And the guilt was horrendous.

Right now, though, she had to get home. Pulling into her driveway, she was a little sad, no, just disappointed, to see her note gone off the door. He'd been and gone. Okay. She didn't want to see him anyway. He was everything she didn't want. A male who thought he could be the boss of her. Who thought he could spank her, of all the degrading things! She could have stayed home, answered to a headship, and had that for the rest of her life if that was what she wanted. It wasn't what she wanted.

Getting out of the car, she walked to the door and unlocked it. Then heading to the laundry room to see her dogs, she firmly disregarded the thought of him spanking her, cuddling her and then discussing things with her as an adult. It made no sense in her brain. Not one bit of sense at all. But a lot of things she did didn't make sense either.

Just like her hiding her non-drinking. There was no reason to pretend to drink or to discreetly order a non-alcoholic version of a drink. She could just tell people she didn't drink, but felt they would judge her. Like she always felt judged wearing matching dresses to church. She and her sisters always wore the same things when they went out. Their mom said it saved money, because all she had to do was make one new dress or jumper as they grew, and everyone else could wear a hand me down. Also she could keep track of them as they walked down the street like a circus freak show. She'd noticed, but never said the boys didn't have to do that. Their shirts didn't have to all match, they could wear comfortable jeans. Why? Were they more important? Thoughts for another day.

"Hello, my babies," she said, opening the laundry room door. "You two want to go for a walk and then go to bed early with me tonight? I feel like curling up with people who love me." They both looked at her and she smiled. She knew they loved her and she would do her best for them. "Let's go for a walk and discuss our weekend, okay? We will have a good time, just us girls. We will go shopping, we will buy us some treats, we might have pedicures together, who knows?" Snapping their leash on, they headed out into the warm summer air.

She planned to enjoy the next few days before she started the new job on Wednesday. It would be very different from anything she'd done before, and she knew Ellie, who would be her boss, was nervous about it. They would learn together, though. Being a right-hand man came easily and naturally to her. She always picked up a new job's requirements quickly, but then got bored, wanted another challenge and moved on. To be honest with herself, she thought as she stopped to watch the puppies sniff the neighbor's bush, she hadn't left her job at Max's office because of wanting a new challenge.

She wanted to get out of there because of her comfort level. It was just too much to work with Max every day, and she didn't want to think about why. She'd jumped into another job too quickly and honestly it had bored her from day two, once she found the way to the break room and put names to faces. Being glad that Ellie had offered her another job was an understatement. Lucy couldn't imagine being the city manager's assistant would be boring. She'd never followed politics like Ellie had, so there would be a lot to learn.

"Do you two want to go to the dog park tomorrow and then go to the puppy store and get some treats?" she asked them as they came back into the house. "Mommy is going to take a nice hot shower while you eat supper and then we can go to bed and watch TV. How's that sound?"

They seemed to agree, but she hoped they wouldn't fight over what movie to see. Some horrible B level disaster movie sounded good. Last thing she wanted was watching a giggly couple search for their forever home, or even worse, a rom-com. Yeah. She needed a big scary monster who wanted to eat the world. That would make things better in her brain, pretty sure.

Max pulled his car into Lucy's driveway early Monday morning. He had about five hours before he was scheduled to go into work, and planned to spend the morning with her. First he'd see how Gypsy was, and then they would discuss that note on the door. Then he would feed her the donuts he'd picked up on the way over and hopefully have a good time. Not in bed, unless, well, no unless. He'd made a vow. He was going to romance the girl for at least three months before he made a move. At that point, both of them should know more of what they wanted or didn't want from each other. He owed it to her, and maybe to himself to try this romance thing. What would it hurt? He'd done stupider things.

Knocking on the door, he heard the yips from two little dogs and smiled. His girl had taken care of his other girl well this weekend, it sounded like.

"Come on in!" she called. He opened the unlocked door and came in with his donut bag. "I wasn't expecting you for a couple hours." She looked adorably dismayed, in her little shorts, oversized t-shirt, bare feet and now gold blonde hair flying everywhere.

"Obviously," he said walking in. "What are you doing?"

"Making you a surprise," she said. "Well, Gypsy is. I was going to do it with Juliet anyway, but since Gypsy was here…"

He looked at the table, covered in some kind of brown paper and a bucket, a couple pans and he didn't have a clue what the rest of it was. She had a smudge of something that looked like flour on her face and looked at him with such disappointment, he almost laughed but fought it down.

"Well, since I ruined the surprise, what is it?"

"If I tell you, will you pretend to be surprised on Christmas morning?"

"I promise," he said, solemnly, fighting a smile. Would they be together on Christmas morning? He wouldn't think about that now.

"We are making pawprint ornaments," she told him. "I plan to do one every year with Juliet and getting her a little tree of her own, filled with ornaments she and I made together. And well, I thought you might like Gypsy's pawprint, too."

She looked at him expectantly as if she wanted him to say something.

"That will be a very wonderful surprise on Christmas morning. I won't have a clue how she managed to do that for me."

"Good," she beamed at him. "You can help me clean up! But don't look at them! They have to dry and I can't move them till they do."

"I will try really hard not to look," he said, putting down the donut bag and picking up his dog. She was more than enough to look at. Gypsy, he assured himself, not the long-legged beauty in front of him. He snuggled his little dog close, then put her down. "What can I do? Then we need to have a talk."

"Oh, do we?" she said, looking at him. "You can dump the

water outside. It's all pasty, put it in the rocks by the bushes, please."

He did as he was told and then ran some water in the bucket to clean it out. Why did she have to be all sweet and adorable when he had plans to put her over his knee and teach her about locking her doors and being safe? Had she done it on purpose?

It didn't change anything, he assured himself. The lesson needed taught. The idea of someone coming in and hurting her because she announced to the world where her key was, was simply unacceptable. Plus the door was unlocked this morning. What was wrong with her? Clearwater was a fairly safe little town, but like every town, they had their share of kids running wild looking to get into trouble, and some just rotten people. He couldn't stand the idea of his little Lucy running into one of them.

Max paused as he carried the bucket back in the house. His? What was he thinking? Sure, he thought he'd try a little romance thing and see where it led. It might not lead anywhere at all, or it might turn into more. But he owed it to both of them to try and figure it out. She seemed amiable to the idea, so why not? It wasn't like he had anyone else on the radar, and really hadn't since he'd watched her drag that huge pine tree into the office. Watching Mike's vein bulge in his forehead was just a little perk.

He came back in smiling and shaking his head. Didn't mean she was going to get out of a lesson, though.

"What are we doing Wednesday night?" she asked him. He noticed she had almost everything cleaned up already. The woman had energy for so early in the morning.

"Want to go to Angel's for Italian or The Rusty Nail for barbeque?" he asked her, grabbing a towel to wipe the bottom of the bucket.

"Surprise me," she said, putting away the last of the things she had scattered everywhere and taking the bucket from him. "I love a surprise!"

"I will do that, but right now we need to have a talk."

"How did your meeting go?" she asked him. "I assume that is what you want to talk about. Do you need some help with paperwork or anything? Bryan is really good. You can rely on him, but I'm glad to help if you need it?" She looked at him expectantly.

Those eyes, he thought.

Amused again, he shook his head. "The meeting went fine, I got the contract and yes, Bryan can handle it. You concentrate on your new job."

Lucy shook her head. He liked that color. Well, he liked all the colors her hair came in. He guessed he liked surprises, too. "I don't start till Wednesday and..." She stopped talking and looked at him.

"And what?" he asked. What was going on in that head?

"And nothing," she said in a way he knew meant and something.

"Lucy, don't you lie to me," he warned.

She sighed, and looked away from him, then said softly and very meekly, "And I don't have any trouble picking up new job duties." She busied herself wiping down the already clean counter. "I've read up on what I'll be doing and what Ellie will be doing, and well, I'll manage."

"Lucy?" Max felt confused and not just in a what was it with women kind of way, but in a real, that was weird, kind of way. He folded his arms and waited. Obviously, she was scrambling to come up with an answer.

"Guys don't like smart women," she finally came out with.

"Who the hell told you that?" he asked. This wasn't the fifties. Females didn't have to pretend to be stupid to get a guy. Did they? He tried to remember if he was ever put off by a smart woman. Not even in elementary school.

She looked at her feet and then at the cloth she kept wiping the counter with. "Everyone knows that. Don't show how smart you are. Men have, well…" she paused again.

This was like pulling teeth, he thought. "Lucy, tell me now."

"Men have fragile egos and if you are smarter than they are or know more, they get upset," she said in one breath.

Max laughed out loud and she glared at him. "Hey, I didn't make the rules!"

"Get your rule abiding butt over here." He sat down on a kitchen stool and pulled her in front of him, between his legs.

Tipping her chin up to look in his eyes, he said, "One, that is crap. Sure, we have egos, but so do women. Smart isn't a pie. If you are smart, that doesn't make me less smart, or the guy in the cubicle next to you. Understand?"

Lucy shrugged a little. "I guess." The doubt, however, was very thick in her voice.

He suddenly had a thought. "Is that why you job hop? So no one figures out how smart you really are?"

Dropping her eyes, Lucy shrugged again. "Maybe," she whispered, squirming to get away, and obviously uncomfortable. He clamped his legs around her thighs. No, she wasn't squirming out of this. His mind raced. Ellie had dropped hints Lucy had a messed-up background, but he suspected he didn't even know the first thing about how messed up it was. However, that wasn't the point right now.

Sighing, he said, "Okay, that's a conversation for another day and we will be talking about it. Right now, we are going to talk about your front door."

"What?" She cocked her head at him and tried to take a step backwards, but he wasn't letting her go anywhere.

"I dropped Gypsy off the other day," he said.

"I told you where the key was and you obviously found it and got in," she said.

"Obviously. And today when I came the door was unlocked."

"I just got back from walking the dogs and then got busy doing, you know, the Christmas surprise." Lucy flipped her hair. "I don't understand."

"Crime is a thing," he said, slowly so she would understand.

"What does that have to do with me?" she asked, still trying to squirm away. He had her caught though. She wasn't going anywhere. Except the best place to enforce a lesson.

"Lucy, you put a sign on your front door announcing where you left the key. You probably would have been safer just leaving the door unlocked without the note."

She cocked her head at him, apparently confused. "I didn't leave it unlocked."

"No, but think. What if I parked downtown, left the keys in the car while I went in shopping? Left a note on the window saying, 'key is in the car'. What do you think might happen?"

She looked at him, then lowered her eyes again. "The car would be gone, I guess."

"What if I was walking by your house and saw the note on the door? Someone could have found the key before me and been in here waiting for you, or cleaned out your house before you got home. Lucy, that was very dangerous."

"I had to go, I had an appointment. You had a timeline. You had to get in. It seemed practical." She seemed to think that was the end of the conversation and tried, again, to pull away.

"Lucy, why didn't you text me and tell me where the key was?"

"I guess I could have done that." She nodded and then smiled. "Okay. I will do that next time. I promise."

She was entirely missing the point. He gave up and pulled

her over one of his knees so her adorable, very spankable bottom was perched right over it.

"Hey! I said I wouldn't do it again!" she protested, trying to get up. He clamped his leg over her two effectively trapping her and giving him a wonderful target for the spanking he was about to give.

"You need an object lesson in being safe," he said, partly wondering if she really did or if he just wanted to spank her. Did it matter? Not really. She was getting a spanking in any case. Just because he wanted to spank her and what better reason was there? And she deserved one for not thinking about locking her doors.

He smacked her bottom. "Settle down and quit fighting. You are getting a spanking and there is nothing you can do about it."

"I can bite your leg," she warned.

"You do and you won't sit down for a week or longer," he said, trying not to smile. "Think how you'd explain that at your new job."

"Let me up, Maxwell Jeremiah Sutherland! I mean it! Right now!"

How did she know his middle name? No one knew his middle name, for obvious reasons. He smacked her bottom, hard, making her squeal.

"Just a little something to help you remember to lock your door and be safe. You need to take care of you."

"Let me up! I do take care of me! Who else would?"

"Me, obviously." He smacked her again, and enjoyed her reaction as she tried to buck and twist, but could go nowhere, even her hands flailed around, not helping her cause at all. "I will make sure you are taken care of."

What was he thinking? Of course he would, but still. He smacked her on top of her soft cotton shorts and wished he'd yanked her pants down before he started. In this position it would be challenging. More for the visual than for anything else. They weren't really protection for her poor, soon to be sore bottom.

However, it hurt his heart a little that she thought no one would take care of her. He was about to dissuade her of that nonsense right now. He smacked her again, four times, just to get her warmed up.

"You remember this next time you feel like leaving your door unlocked or announcing to the world where your key is." He started smacking her quickly while she howled in protest.

"Max! Stop it! I don't want this!"

"I don't want you getting hurt," he said.

"So you spank me? It hurts! Stop it!" He could hear her voice rising and knew he was getting her attention.

"Spankings are supposed to hurt. It helps you remember," he said, not stopping his steady one-two-three-four rhythm on her wiggling bottom. Next time those pants were coming off for sure. That thought made him smile despite her distress.

"I remember!" she shrieked. "Let me up! Ow! Okay, no more!"

"We are just getting warmed up," he told her as she pounded her fist against his leg.

"I won't have you unsafe," he said, his last word punctuated with a hard smack on her sweet sit spot making her screech.

"Ow! I won't be! I promise! No no! Please!"

That was better.

"Max! Stop it! Okay, no more!"

She sure talked a lot for someone who was getting her little butt warmed. Apparently she could handle more if her mouth could run like that.

"Max! Please! I'll be good!"

"You will be good," he agreed, but didn't stop his steady smacks on her backside. This felt, oddly, right to him. He didn't question why, but just knew somehow this was where she belonged. Squalling like a scalded cat over his lap, getting her little rear warmed up. Yeah.

"Please! I'm sorry! I'm sorry!" That last word hit a high note so he doubled down in that spot. "No! No! Not there! Okay, okay! I understand it!"

Finally, after he heard her let out a few hard sobs, he stopped and started rubbing her bottom, waiting for her to calm down.

"What did you learn?" he asked after a minute when he felt her start to relax.

"Never to leave you any notes!"

"Smart mouth brat," he told her, smacking her once more just to hear her squeal again, and then moved his leg so she could scramble off his lap. She stood in front of him, red faced, teary eyes, tousled hair, and frantically rubbing her bottom and he thought she was the prettiest thing he'd ever seen. What was wrong with him today?

"Now, who is going to lock her door?"

She glared at him and stuck her lip out in a pout that made him want to kiss her thoroughly. "Me," she said, reluctance thick in her voice.

"Good girl," he said. "Now, blow your nose and tell me thank you."

"For what?" She blew her nose but didn't take her eyes off his.

"For enforcing a lesson you won't forget and that you will be safe from now on. Or do you need a little more to help you remember?"

"No, Sir!" she said quickly, tossing her tissue and rubbing her bottom again. "I'll remember."

"And?" he prompted.

"Thank you for my lesson," she mumbled, finally dropping her eyes.

"You are very welcome, and since you took your lesson so well, I'll take you somewhere special Wednesday, how about that?"

Her eyes met his again. "You are still taking me out?"

"Of course I am. We have a date, remember?"

"I just thought…" Her voice trailed away as he pulled her between his legs again, into a hug. She all but melted into him and he smiled. Yeah, this was what he liked. Her sweet compliant body against him.

"Just because you need a spanking once in a while doesn't mean I'm going back on my word about the romance thing I promised you," he said. Who would have thought he actually meant words like that? He sure seemed to, though. He was getting soft in his old age.

"Spankings aren't very romantic," she grumbled.

"Romance comes in many forms," he kissed the top of her head. "You will find out. Now, I need to get my dog and get to work. Thank you very much for watching her. Where are her meds?"

"Right here," she reached in the cabinet and handed the sack over. "Thank you for letting me have her for a few days. I've missed her."

And I have missed you, he almost said out loud but stopped himself. Too much too fast. Take it slow, he reminded himself. This one not only needed a firm hand on the rear, but a gentle one on her emotions and her obviously agile brain. It would be fun. Or something.

"What are you going to do when I leave?" he asked her.

"Stick my tongue out at you after I lock the door?" she asked, and rubbed her bottom again.

"That works. You have a good couple of days and I will pick you up Wednesday night about six." He laughed as he walked out to his car.

Lucy locked the door after him, but didn't bother to stick

her tongue out at him. What was wrong with her? He deserved it. She rubbed her bottom again, it didn't hurt anymore, but stung some. Why did he do that to her and why didn't she resent him and vow to never speak to him again? Why did it make her want to be close to him? Why did it feel like Wednesday was six days away instead of the day after tomorrow?

Hearing her phone ring, she found it on her counter. "Hey, Ellie," she answered it. "How are things there today?"

"Laid back. Did Gypsy go home yet?"

Lucy rubbed her bottom again. "She did, why?"

"I want to go shopping for a first day of work suit and then get a mani-pedi. Apparently I'm going to be on TV again Wednesday and my nails need to be sublime. Want to come along?"

Lucy had big plans to clean out her laundry room and vacuum today, but decided to bravely overcome that little obstacle. "I'd love to! Want to come get me or want me to meet you somewhere?"

"I'll head your way in a couple hours. See you then!" Maybe she would pick up something for her date Wednesday night? Couldn't hurt to look anyway.

"Hear that, Juliet? I'm going shopping!"

Chapter 4

Lucy smiled as she snapped on Juliet's leash so they could go for a walk before she left on her date with Max. She'd had a good morning text from him, where he'd confirmed the time this evening, but nothing the rest of the day. That was fine because she'd been crazy busy learning at work. It had been wonderful. She loved a challenge and that was what she had in front of her. Apparently the last admin had left her a mess to clean up. She didn't mind. Cleaning up messes was kind of what she'd been bred to do, after all. Sure, her folks meant other kinds of messes, like diapers and spilled milk, but still. This kind was preferable. Numbers and paperwork and computer programs. Fun times and a wonderful mental challenge.

Lucy felt a little guilty that she hoped it was a really bad mess. When the last city manager left, all his staff had quit, too. She and Ellie were starting from scratch with no help or input at all. Ellie seemed a little overwhelmed but she was excited. Of course, she wasn't the face of the city manager, just a small behind the scenes worker. Being the face was all on Ellie. And why she let Ellie talk her into this dress, she wasn't sure. It was a little tight and a little short, and well, there was a little too much cleavage. It didn't feel like a date night dress to her, but really, it probably had to be. She sighed. Why could men get away with wearing comfy clothes when all she'd be doing all night was holding her stomach in? They'd been talking about Max when she tried it on at the store. She and Ellie always shared everything. Well, almost everything. She hadn't told Ellie that Max spanked her, but did tell her Max had figured out her big secret, the one only Ellie knew.

"Your IQ?" Ellie asked. "How did he find that out? You know I've never understood why you try and hide your brilliance, but I know you do."

"I don't know," Lucy said. "I guess I was just feeling close to him and somehow he managed to figure it out." Ellie assumed they'd been in bed, instead of her standing there, rubbing her freshly paddled rear end. Well, weird as it was, she had been feeling close to him then, and vulnerable and for some reason, it had just happened. She did feel a little embarrassed about it, but wasn't sure why. Ellie had tried to assure her it was no big deal, that nothing would change, but Lucy wasn't sure. She needed to be a little more careful and make sure he didn't find anything else out.

"For a job-hopping airhead, you sure have a lot of secrets," she told the mirror as she finished applying a light coat of makeup.

Lucy didn't bother with jewelry, the dress was more than enough. While it had long sleeves, her shoulders were bare. It was a dark blue with white fringe on the plunging neckline and just under the cut-out sleeves. It wasn't anything she usually wore, but this wasn't just any night, was it? She was celebrating her first day on her new job! And she rarely splurged on dress up clothes, preferring to focus her wardrobe on office basics and comfy home clothes, but that was why she worked. To enjoy life and splurge a little. This dress had been a little more than a little, but it wasn't like she splurged often. The red dress she wore to Ellie's party had been ten bucks at the thrift store. This one had been full price at the fancy store and she still wasn't sure why. Well, it was to celebrate her new job.

Yes, that was all it was, a splurge for a new job celebration. Shoes. Black didn't go well with navy blue, she didn't think, anyway, so she slipped on a pair of low-heeled red pumps. Good enough. She fluffed her hair and went to lock Juliet in the laundry room till she got back. "In a few more months, you'll be able to sleep on the couch while I'm gone," she cooed to her. "We will give that housebreaking thing a little longer, though."

She picked her up, but then heard the doorbell. "I guess you get a couple minute reprieve," she told her. "Let's go let Max in."

They walked to the door, and opened it. Lucy's mouth dropped open as she saw what he had in his hand. "Happy first day of work," he told her, handing the dozen peach colored roses to her.

Speechless, Lucy stepped back. "Oh, wow, Max. They are, they are…"

He shut the door behind him as she buried her nose in the roses. "They smell so good." She sniffled a little bit as she turned to go find something to put them in. Did she even own a vase?

"Lucy? Are you crying?" he asked.

Not answering or looking at him, she simply said, "I've never had flowers before."

"Never?"

She shook her head and found a gallon jar she usually made tea in, to put her flowers in. Her flowers and they were gorgeous! "Thank you. I love them." Finally, she looked at him and smiled. He looked good. "You clean up well, you know," she told him.

"Thank you, ma'am," he said. "I'm glad you're pleased. You look amazing, in case no one has told you today."

"No one has!" she said, and gave the roses one more sniff. "You shouldn't have, but thank you."

"Your prom date didn't bring you a corsage?" he asked.

Lucy giggled. "I didn't go to prom," she told him. "I didn't date till college."

Max shook his head. "You deserve many flowers in your future," he told her. "You ready to go?"

Lucy nodded and picked Juliet up from the floor again, and put her in the laundry room with her bed, food and water. "Let me wash my hands and grab my purse," she told him. Grabbing her white shrug and her purse, she went to the kitchen to sniff her roses one more time, then asked, "Where are we going?"

"There's a new seafood place opening up at the edge of town," he said. "Tonight is their soft opening and I thought we'd try it before word got out."

"How did you find out?" she asked, being very careful to lock the door behind them as they left.

"One of my clients owns it," he said. "She invited me. I think her son is the chef."

"That sounds great," Lucy said. "Thank you." She slid into the car after he opened the door. Had to watch the way you got in a car with a dress this short, she reminded herself.

"You look very nice, too," she told him after he got in. "And your car smells good."

It did. Like, leather or something.

"Had it detailed just for you," he told her.

Laughing, Lucy looked out her window. "Did not. I used to work with you. You have it detailed a couple times a month."

"Dang, woman, is there anything you don't know?"

"Probably not," she said. "Gotta be on your best behavior with me."

"I'll try," he said. "So tell me about your first day at work? Think you are going to like it?"

Lucy chattered about the new job as they drove through their pretty little town. "And my favorite part," she wound up as he pulled into the half full restaurant parking lot, "is that the offices all close at four! It seems so much earlier than five or five thirty, for some reason."

"Government jobs," he said, unbuckling his seat belt. "You get all the perks."

"Well, it's great now, in the summer when there is so much light, but it will be even better this winter. Getting out of there before it gets too dark in the evenings. It is a wonderful perk," she agreed. "Plus all the sick pay and benefits, it's a really nice job."

"Stay there," he warned as he got out of the car and walked around to open her door. She thought it was a silly thing to do, but really, it made her feel a little warm and mushy inside when he did that for her. "So do you think you will stay there a while?"

Lucy shrugged as she slipped her hand in his to walk across the parking lot. "Who knows? I'll stay as long as Ellie needs me, probably, but really, I guess I'll find out. I usually know when it is time to leave."

"You might, but no one ever knows your thought process," he said, as he opened the door to the restaurant. It sure didn't look like one of those chain seafood places with the cheesy fish on the walls and the people dressed up as pretend pirates. This was very upscale.

There was a large water feature just to the side of the hostess station that gurgled and trickled happily. She liked it, and the sound. The walls were a dark sea blue and the tables and booths covered in crisp white cloths. She didn't think she'd ever been to a restaurant with tablecloths before. How much laundry did they go through?

"Welcome to The Running Water," greeted a hostess dressed in black. "Two of you? Would you like a booth or a table?"

"Booth please," Max said, and she followed him to the booth. While very formal, it seemed comfortable here. Like a place she and her friends could come and have a few drinks, with appetizers and laughs. The booths were large and comfortable. Six of them could easily sit in one.

"May I start you off with a cocktail?" Their server asked a few minutes later.

"White wine for me and sparkling water with lemon for the lady," he said. Lucy smiled at him, happily.

"Thank you," she said, pleased he remembered she didn't drink and that she didn't have to handle the decision. He was comfortable to be with tonight and she liked that.

She chattered on about her job till the salads arrived, and then stopped with her fork part way to her mouth. Oh, heck no.

"Hello, Miranda," she said as the woman simply slid into the booth beside Max. He obligingly moved over as if he expected her. She had nothing against Miranda George, she reminded herself. She had done a great job decorating Ellie's new house, despite the fact Miranda and Ellie's husband, Mike had dated for a while and had what appeared to be a very messy break up. Lucy's beef with her, probably, was she was entirely too comfortable with Max. Touchy feely, and getting too close to him and acting as if they were best friends. She didn't like that and for some reason, she didn't like it a lot. It wasn't Miranda, she assured herself. It was the naughty things Miranda did. For some reason that made a difference. Supposedly.

"I was so surprised when I saw the two of you from across the room. I never in a hundred years thought I'd see you both here this evening! What are the odds you'd be invited on opening night!" Miranda moved a little closer to Max and Lucy tried not to frown at her. Being friendly, or friends, was not a crime, she reminded herself.

Was it her imagination or had Miranda developed a southern accent since she'd seen her last, at Ellie's house warming party a few months back?

"What are you doing here tonight, Miranda?" Max asked, putting his fork down. "Haven't seen you in a while."

Well, that was good to know, Lucy thought as she smiled at her but finished putting her forkful of salad in her mouth.

"Oh, I decorated the place," Miranda said. "Didn't you know? My first big business client and I'm just thrilled. Don't you think the place looks fantastic?"

Lucy nodded. Okay, she could give her that. "It looks wonderful," she agreed. "You do very good work."

"I'm so happy you think so," Miranda said. "Now that you are working for the city, you can let me know if any opportunities come up there. I can certainly work on a hefty government budget." She laughed, tossing her red-gold hair back, and brushing way too close to Max. "And you know I can't wait to get my hands on your office, right?"

"Not up to me," Max said. "Up to Mike, so I doubt that will happen."

"Well, you never know. Nora and Ernie were so pleased with my work here, they gave me a free meal here every week for the next year and a special invitation for tonight. Wasn't that wonderful!"

"I hope that was on top of paying you." Lucy couldn't help herself. It slipped out.

"Of course it was, dear. I don't give my work away. Oh, my date is here. I'll see you soon, Max. Bye, Lucy."

Lucy watched her walk away and said, "She comes and goes so quickly."

"Not quickly enough," Max said. "Hope she didn't ruin your appetite."

Lucy stabbed her salad and said, "She means nothing to me. Why would she?" Then stuck the forkful of vegetables in her mouth. And chewed. Then did it again. "I hope she does well with her business," she finally said.

Max pushed his almost empty salad plate aside. "I think she's doing pretty well," he said. "How about you? How are you doing?"

"Me?" Lucy cocked her head and looked at him. "What do you mean me? It's only day one of this job and all I've done all night is talk about it. You know how it's going."

He looked uncomfortable but said, "Thank you," as the server removed their salad plates. He picked up his drink and took a sip. Then looked at her and said, "You quit working for us a few months ago."

"I had a job to go to." Where was he going with this? "I thought you understood."

"You change jobs, often," he said.

Lucy had no idea what he was talking about. "I haven't been unemployed since I started college. I always have a new job to go to before I give notice on the other job. I don't understand."

"Be careful, they are hot," the woman in black put down sizzling plates in front of them. Oh, that smelled good. He had scallops, sea bass, twice baked potato, asparagus and a yeasty smelling dinner roll. She had ordered a spiced cauliflower steak with lemon, herb and toasted almond. This was worth the trip.

"I happen to know what you made in the job you just left was about half of what you made with us," Max said.

Lucy picked up her utensils and sliced a bit of her

cauliflower steak. Okay. She got it. She put the bite in her mouth and chewed deliberately, trying to calm down before she answered him. Why did he bring out the worst in her? But he did and she was going to put him in his place.

"You want to know if I'm hurting for money because I'm just a little air-headed blonde who can't handle her life." It was a statement, not a question.

"Lucy, no. That isn't what I meant at all," he said. "But if you are short till the checks start coming in, well, you don't have to worry."

"I bought a new dress for this date," she informed him. "It wasn't cheap. I got a new puppy. Neither of those are inexpensive nor desperately needed. If I was hurting would I be doing that?"

Was she leftover mad because of Miranda? It was a simple misunderstanding and he was trying to help. Nothing more. She should be happy and grateful he thought enough of her to offer to help. However, she felt hurt and upset and wasn't really sure why. She ate in silence for several minutes while contemplating her next statement. The food here was really good, she noted, wondering if Jordyn knew the chef. She'd have to ask her next time she saw her.

He didn't say anything either, but ate steadily. She hoped he was very uncomfortable and finally decided to put him out of his misery.

"Max, is your car paid for?" she asked. This was going to be fun.

"Will be by the end of the year," he said.

"Mine is. Is your house paid for?"

"My house?" he asked. "No, my condo isn't paid for."

"Mine is." she said. "I have also hit my contribution limit for my 401K for the year, and what is it? August?"

Then Lucy put a bite of yeast roll in her mouth. It was wonderful. She'd have to see if Jordyn had a recipe for them that she could teach her to make. Hers never turned out this wonderfully. Maybe it was the commercial kitchen. Hopefully, it was a recipe.

"You know I'm not the airhead people think I am. We discussed that before, despite my reservations about telling anyone. Well, one of my first jobs was working for an investment banker, sort of like what you and Mike do." She put her fork down and dabbed her lips with her thick, heavy cloth napkin and smiled sweetly at him while she tossed her blonde hair and affected her airhead look. She had it down pat. "Anything you can do, I can do better. Including investing money and day trading."

"Not everything," he assured her, seemingly unbothered by her financial prowess. That was good, right? "I'm glad I don't have to spot you five."

"You're welcome." She tried to calm down. *Keep Sweet*, she reminded herself. That is what girls did. Never let anyone see or know any emotions, except happiness and compliance.

"So how are your veggies?" he asked her. "My food is excellent."

"Everything here is wonderful," she said. "Thank you so much for bringing me, I'm having a good time." Was she? She wasn't sure. Between Miranda snuggling him, and him trying to turn her into a charity case, well, the food was good. And he was very easy on the eyes. Focus on the good, Lucy reminded herself. Besides, he brought her flowers. That gave him an extra few brownie points.

"There is a lot about you I don't know, isn't there?" he asked her, later, over the best lemon cake she'd ever had.

Lucy giggled, the sugar and full stomach making her feel better. Not all the way better, but enough so she could fake it well. "Why, yes, sir, there is," she said. "Just like I imagine there is a lot about you I don't know."

"Not that much," he said and looked at his watch. "Are you almost done?"

Nodding, Lucy put her last bite of cake in her mouth. Jordyn needed this recipe, too.

"Good," he waved the server down and handed her his credit card. "We have a place to be."

"A place to be?" she echoed. Okay, it was still early. He tucked her into the car and headed back to town. "Where are we going?" she asked.

"You will see. You like surprises," he reminded her, shooting her a smile.

"Yeah." Lucy felt an edge of anticipation. Hopefully, this would be fun. If not, then she'd ask him to take her home, or walk. She could walk in these shoes for a few miles.

He pulled into the town square and parked along the edge. "Come on," he said, pulling her out of the car. " Let's go dance."

"Dance?" There wasn't a bar downtown that had live music. There were just a couple cafes and diners.

"Yup." They walked toward the town square.

There in Central Park where every year the town Christmas tree went up, Santa set up his off-site office for the kids, the charity events were held, and the… "Oh! The high school band is playing tonight!"

"Yes, ma'am," he said. "And we are going dancing."

Giggling in anticipation, Lucy let him pull her through the crowd to a small area under a few trees to the side of where the band had set up and were already playing the first number.

"Do you dance?" he asked her.

"I do not dance, but I know I'm a good follower," she told him, "and apparently I need to be to dance."

"Yes, ma'am," he smiled at her. "You are and you do. Come here, I'll lead our way." She stepped into his outstretched arms and for the next hour, he taught her to dance to the tune of a high school band's melodies. She couldn't remember ever having more fun.

"A dozen peach roses, dancing, and dinner at the swanky new place in town, and he didn't want anything more than a kiss good night? Umm, so what are you thinking?" Ellie looked at her as if she expected her to know something. It had been a few days since her date, but this was the first alone time they'd had together.

"I'm totally baffled," Lucy admitted. "But really, I had the best time. And he wants to see me again Saturday afternoon. Ellie, you get men, what's going on?"

"You think I get men?" Ellie took a bite of her orange chicken and laughed.

"Well, you are married, you have to understand something about them!" Lucy insisted. "I have no clue. You know, he's my, well, you know." *First.*

"I know, which makes it weirder. Once they get, well, you know, they keep expecting it," Ellie said, and twisted in her office chair, then reached over and grabbed another egg roll. Working lunch, they'd decided that morning. Ellie had a lot of questions about the finances of the city, and Lucy had a lot of questions about the male psyche. They needed some best friend/sister time and if a working lunch was all the time they had, then it worked.

Lucy sighed as she dipped her egg roll into the sauce. All she'd ever been told was she had to have one of those male things in her life, to be her leader and knock her up, and all they wanted was a compliant sweet doll to cook their food, warm their beds and birth their babies. Nothing more and nothing less. Sure, other women held jobs and they worked with them, but they weren't worthy women, the kind you married. Those kind, the good ones, were at home with their parents, studying their religious texts and raising their siblings in preparation for raising their own kids after they got married.

"Sometimes I think I'm doing okay, and then sometimes I fall right back into my raising," she told Ellie, who nodded as if she understood. Lucy knew she did intellectually, but really, she couldn't. She'd been raised to do anything she wanted and even her bossy big brother and bossy husband had no intention of quelching her ambitions. Lucy had been raised for one thing. You grew up, got married, and had as many babies for the quiver as you could till your body gave out or you aged out. The end. No one realized how hard it had been to leave or how easy it was to slip back into that way of thinking.

Her college therapist had helped her a lot, as had Ellie's grandma and Ellie herself, as an example of how Lucy thought 'normal' people acted. One of Ellie's greatest gifts was empathy. She loved and accepted. Her other greatest gift, or talent, was her ambition.

"I'm just confused, Ellie," she said. Lucy longed to tell her about the spankings. How they made her feel, other than the pain, but the vulnerability, the closeness she felt to him, the security she felt knowing he would do it if he said he would. The knowledge that just because she messed up, or upset him, that after a spanking, he wasn't leaving her.

Until he did, of course.

So many emotions she couldn't even name them, much less speak them out loud. And really, who wanted to admit to another grown adult they got their butt paddled? It just wasn't done. No, some things were kept private, even from your best friend.

Spankings were one of those things.

They finished their Chinese food and cleaned up, then Ellie said, "So, let's talk finances."

Lucy grinned, even though it wasn't the least bit amusing. "Yes. Let's, 'cause there sure is something funky going on somewhere."

"Just what I need to tell Mayor Lydia," Ellie said, then sighed. "But, better than not telling her."

"My opinion is, we figure out what happened and be able to present her with actual figures and information instead of going to her with wild speculation." Lucy wiped her fingers on a napkin, then picked up a file folder. "I have a feeling we are only at the tip of the glacier."

"Is it going to be bad?" Ellie asked her.

"Someone was skimming for sure, for many years and it adds up to a lot of the taxpayers' money," Lucy told her. No wonder everyone had quit when the last city manager left. If it was her, she not only would have left, but she would have skipped town and maybe the country before someone found out all this mess. How did they think she wouldn't find out? Well, they didn't know her.

"How could you have possibly found this out in just a few days?" Ellie asked, going over the files.

"I read fast," Lucy said. "But really, I have to do more digging. We have nothing concrete yet. I mean, it happened, but I have yet to follow the entire paper and computer trail. I should know more in a few days, if you are comfortable waiting that long to inform anyone."

Ellie looked at the file again. "Okay, I'm going to tell Lydia you found some issues with the bookkeeping and we are looking into it. That we should have a report if something did or didn't happen in a few days. Is that okay with you? I just need someone to know we are the ones looking into it, not the ones who created it."

Lucy nodded. "Ellie, it really wouldn't hurt to have Sheriff

Graham at that meeting with Lydia, too if you really want to cover our butts."

Ellie nodded but looked a little nervous. "I will, if you think it is a good idea. Can you set it up for me as soon as possible?"

"No problem," Lucy said. "And I can go with you, if needed."

Ellie sighed. "Okay, you go for it. I give you any kind of permission you need to find out, and then as soon as you get things gathered, let me know. I'm leaving it in your very capable hands. Now, what kind of meetings do I have scheduled for this afternoon and with whom?"

Lucy walked back to her own little office later, thinking about the file she'd found. She did read fast, but someone had left it in a locked drawer in her desk, almost as if they wanted her to find it. Once she read what was in it, she couldn't stop looking, and like she told Ellie, she knew she hadn't uncovered most of it yet. What a notch in Ellie's belt it would be if the new, youngest, first female, city manager unearthed widespread corruption in the courthouse? Her political career would soar. And she would be right there to watch her friend fly.

"We are doing what?" Lucy giggled, glad he told her to wear her sneakers.

"Going to the petting zoo," he said as he opened the car door for her. "Have you ever been?"

Their town had a very nice, from what she heard, small little zoo that had been upgraded a few years back. It had been a big deal, at the time. They'd put in a trolley, added an aquarium, and a few other things she didn't remember. She knew it was a great tourist attraction, and took part of the city's budget, but she'd never been there. It just hadn't crossed her mind to go. Several of her friends volunteered out there, but she hadn't been around any animals other than dogs, and had never seen a reason to be. It wasn't something on her radar. "No. I thought it was for kids and preschool classes and things," she said.

"Sure but they let grownups in too. And if you are really good, I will buy you a snow cone."

"What if I'm not really good?" she asked.

"Then you buy me a snow cone," he said, patting her bare leg under the cargo shorts she wore.

"Sounds like a plan," she said, hoping it would be a good time. Well, she was with him and it was an adventure. She could roll with the flow. It would be great, she decided. Fun was all in your brain. Well, mostly in your brain.

"I am actually having the best time," she informed Max an hour later as they stepped into the trolley to take a tour around the zoo. "This is fun. I had no clue this was all hidden back here."

"I can't believe you haven't been here. Growing up, we came out every year or two with our school classes and then of course anytime the cousins came to town, they always begged to go."

"Tell me about your family," Lucy asked as they settled into seats in the back of the open air trolley.

"I have a big family," he said. "Four siblings, and I'm in the middle. A couple dozen cousins, lots of aunts and uncles, two grandmas still around. I'll take you to meet them sometime," he said. "They will adore you."

Would they? Wasn't going home to meet the parents a big step? She wasn't sure she was ready for that!

"Get that look of fear out of your eyes." He patted her leg again. "We aren't going today."

"Oh, okay," she said, feeling relieved. She knew she should

mention her family, but she just didn't want to right now. It was too nice a day to bring things like that up.

"What was your favorite part?" he asked her as they sipped and crunched their grape snow cones as they walked to the car. She must have been good, because he'd paid.

"I'm supposed to say you," she teased, "but it was the baby goats. Who knew baby goats were so cute?"

"They must have thought you were cute, too," he said, pulling out his phone to show her a picture of herself surrounded by a pack of baby goats. Did goats come in packs or herds? She'd have to find out. "They have good taste."

"You are silly." They stopped at a bench to finish their yummy icy treats. "I had such a good time. Thank you for bringing me, today."

"No one I'd rather zoo with," he told her, tossing his paper cup. She saw him look up and his expression changed, so she looked, too. Of course. Her favorite person.

"Why, fancy seeing you two here!" Miranda cooed at them, looking as if she was not ready to go hiking around the zoo and getting baby goat kisses. Instead she had on a figure flattering light-blue dress and white heels, which made her feel very dowdy in her cargo shorts, sneakers and t-shirt.

"Hello, Miranda," Max said and Lucy dutifully parroted it. "What are you doing here?"

"I have an appointment with part of the zoo board. I'm going to be designing the planned expansion to the gift shop. Won't that be fun for everyone?" She flipped her long, red-gold hair back and looked around. "I'm so excited about being part of making this place better and more exciting for families!"

"Well, you will do a great job," Max said. "Sounds like your business is doing very well."

"Was there ever any doubt?" she said, smiling in what Lucy was sure she thought was a disingenuous way. Lucy

MEGAN MCCOY

watched Miranda's body language while she and Max talked. There was something, or had been something, going on between the two of them. She'd been under the impression that Miranda was Mike's ex, not Max's. But watching her, and watching him, well, there was something. There was that meeting in the gazebo at Ellie's house warming party. And how weird was it that she had coincidentally run into them twice now, in two very unusual places?

"Oh, look!" Lucy said, looking out to the parking lot. "There's Jordyn! I'm going to say hi real quick."

She took off across the parking lot where her friend was getting out of her car with her sister and her sister's two kids. "Jordyn!" She called and waved, glad to be away from Miranda. And away from the way Max was when she was around.

"Hey, Lucy! What are you doing here?" Jordyn asked.

"Oh, Max brought me out," she said. "He wanted to see the new exhibits."

"Are they good?" her sister, Stephanie asked, while strapping her toddler twins into a double stroller. "Not that I care. I just need out of the house for a while."

"We're out," Jordyn said, and told Lucy, "Hey, you want to walk through with us? Three adults to two kids is much better odds."

Lucy shook her head. "I have to get back, but you guys have fun! And good luck. Call me later, Jordyn, okay?"

"Will do," Jordyn said, giving her the once over. However, Lucy had heard via the social networking grapevine that Jordyn worked in one of the houses Miranda had recently redecorated. She wanted to learn more about her. About it. The redecorating, of course. Just in case it came up in the course of her job. Something might need decorated. Who knew? She had just started to work, after all!

She wandered slowly back to the bench where Max sat,

now alone, seemingly deep in thought. That didn't bode well, Lucy thought. If Miranda ruined her date, she would not be happy. Not that there was anything she could do about it, of course.

"Hey, Lucy," he said, looking up as she walked up to him, then stood and grabbed her hand. "You ready to clean up and get something to eat? No offense, but you smell like goat."

"I smell like baby goat," she corrected him. "And I like this smell. I might move to the country and get me a pile of goat babies."

"Goat babies grow up to be big goats," he said as they walked to his car, swinging hands like teenagers.

"I guess. I didn't think about that. The big goats were a little scary with their weird eyes. Like they were looking right through you or something," she shivered, despite the heat. "So! What did Miranda want and is she planning on attending all our dates?"

He slammed her car door a little loudly, she thought as he walked around to his side. Should she have even said that? Was he going to be upset with her?

Getting in the car, Max turned part way to face her, put both his hands gently on either side of her face, kissed her nose and said, "Not if I can help it."

Then he kissed her, gently, softly, making her sigh with need. The man knew how to kiss, for sure. He knew how to do other things too, and she wondered if she would ever get that again, as he moved away and said, "Fasten your seatbelt."

Obediently, she did as she was told, and figured why not ask, "So what does she want?"

"I'm not certain," he said. "But once we get cleaned up, we need to talk."

"Should I be scared?" she asked him.

"Well, you haven't deserved a good paddling yet today, so nah, no reason to be," he said.

"Too funny," she said, not smiling. "I've never deserved that!"

"Oh, Lucy, come on now. No reason to lie to yourself," he said, and she could see his lips twitching.

Crossing her arms, she managed a very huffy voice as she said, "I will have you know I am practically perfect in every way! And practically perfect people don't get spanked!"

"Unless they do," he retorted. "Then, it's ass up, over my lap, and let the begging commence."

"That isn't fair," she whined as dramatically as she could. "I mean, what's the point in being practically perfect if you get spanked anyway?"

"Huh. That doesn't seem fair, does it?" he said, pulling into her driveway. "Yet, that's life, isn't it? Not my fault you have a very spankable bottom."

"It isn't my fault either!" She got out of the car before he could come around to open her door. "Dibs on the shower! You get to walk the dogs!" She ran to the door, unlocked it quickly and headed into the bathroom. Her robe was already in there hanging on the hook.

Standing under the running water, she soaped up with her fragrant strawberry mint body wash and scrubbed away the baby goat smell. She'd had a good afternoon with him. Again. Is this what romance was? Dating? Where you went out and had a good time and enjoyed each other and new experiences? Why were her parents dead set against it? Because it was fun? Because that despite how they were raised, they couldn't be trusted not to jump into bed the second a chaperone took their eyes off them? Didn't say much for her folks' raising now, did it, then?

She got out of the shower, dried off and slipped her robe on. She'd get dressed in her bedroom. Max sat on the couch holding the two dogs with a little duffle bag next to him.

"All yours," she said and started to head to the bedroom to get dressed.

"One minute," he said, motioning her to come over.

"Yes?" she asked him, her damp hair falling over her shoulder.

"Do you want your spanking now, or after I shower?" he asked as if that were a serious question.

"What did I do?" she said, stepping back. "I don't want a spanking! You said I didn't do anything to deserve one! No, just no!"

"Well, now if you wanted it, I'd be doing it wrong, wouldn't I? However, it is part of today's date time, so unfortunately, it has to be done. But up to you. Before or after I shower."

"Neither!" she said and fled to her bedroom to get dressed, not sure if she should giggle or be concerned. They had been having such a good time! Okay, though, if he thought he was going to spank her, well... Hearing the shower come on in the next room, she slipped on a bra and a soft, green cotton, short-sleeved blouse. Then went to her panty drawer. Spank her, would he? She pulled out a pair, and put it on. Then another over that and another till they started getting tight after about five pair. She found her favorite soft cotton shorts and put those on. Then a heavier pair of blue jeans shorts. After that, two pairs of sweat pants, and finally her biggest 'bloat' jeans, the pair she wore when she was feeling fat. She had to lie down on the bed to fasten them, but by golly she got them on. Hopefully, she wouldn't need to pee. Her only regret was she didn't own a pair of overalls to wear over them. She'd have to remedy that.

If he wanted to spank her, his hand would be all that was hurting. She'd have to play the part though, she reminded herself. He didn't need to know! Looking in the full-length mirror she thought she might be a little big around the middle but, hey, men didn't notice things like that. She took off her blouse and pulled on an oversized t-shirt. Yes. That worked better. And bonus points, her butt was covered by one more layer.

Oddly, she wasn't really afraid of the pain of the spanking he may or may not really be planning on delivering but more amused and excited. *You are sick*, she told herself, with a big smile. She fluffed her hair, turned on her airhead persona and went to meet her spanker as she heard the shower go off.

He'd put the girls in the laundry room, she noted, Maybe he did mean to spank her. Well, she hadn't done anything naughty, so she wasn't – really – worried. Was she? Nope. Besides. As her college therapist reminded her – protection was a good thing, just in case, and she had protection!

Going behind the island, she opened the fridge and pulled out a couple sodas and then some ice. Getting glasses, she poured them both a drink and sipped hers as she waited for him to come out. Lucy reminded herself to sip slowly. It wouldn't be easy to pull all these down if there was a bathroom emergency!

He came out in clean jeans, a blue t-shirt that was perfection with his dark hair and eyes, toweling off the aforementioned thick dark hair. She handed him the soda as he sat down on the other side of the kitchen island.

So, sir," she said as playfully as she could muster, "since when are spankings part of a romantic date?"

"Since the beginning of time?" he said. "Thank you for the drink."

"Weird, I've never heard that part before," she said. "And I read a lot. And you are welcome."

"Obviously, you don't read the right kinds of books," he said, and placed his drink on her counter. "I'll have to send you over some."

"Maybe I should read them before we proceed to the next

part of the date? Then I'll know what I'm doing." She cocked her head at him and smiled.

"Oh, I'm pretty sure I can walk you through it," he said. "You've been spanked before, just a few days ago in fact."

"That was ten days ago," she interrupted him. "And I've totally forgotten all about it." With that she bit her lip, picked up her soda and sipped from the straw. Is that how you acted provocatively? She was good at book work, but flirt work? Yeah, totally different.

"Have you now?" he asked. "Good thing I'm here to remind you."

"I guess it is," she said. "If I really do need reminded. I might be just fine."

"You are just fine," he said. "You will be finer with a nice warm bottom and a sweet compliant attitude."

Narrowing her eyes at him, she said, "And why do I need either of those?"

"Because I said so." He took another sip of his drink, and stood up.

"Well, that certainly clears that up," she mumbled.

"See how smart you are," he agreed, and held out his hand to her. "Come on, I have reservations at five and we need to get this done."

"Reservations for where?" she asked, suddenly curious. Where were they going that a warm bottom would be needed.

"You'll see," he said, leading her over to the couch. "You like a surprise."

"I like a surprise, but I don't like a spanking," she reminded him as for some reason, she let him walk her to her doom. Or whatever. She still wasn't sure he was really going to do this.

Just a few seconds later, she was no longer in doubt as to his intentions, as he sat down, pulling her face down over his lap in one movement. The man must have practiced that, was her last thought before his hand came down. He had smooth moves.

She felt his confusion and tried not to giggle as she said as convincingly as possible, "Ow! That hurt!"

He smacked her again, this time a little harder and she, once again, cried out, "Ow! No more!" This time the giggle came out with it though.

"Lucy, what did you do?"

"Got ready for my spanking, sir, just like you said to do," she said, trying to bite back her laughter. He smacked her three more times, while she obligingly protested.

He stood her up, and she bit her cheek hard to not smile at him. Now that would have been too cheeky! "Take the shoes off," he said. "Then lose the jeans and get back over my lap."

"Ma-ax" she whined as she kicked off her shoes. Her hands went to her button and she stuck her lip out. "No."

"Now!" Her eyes never leaving his, she slowly pulled her jeans down, then kicked them off and saw him trying not to laugh. "Back over," he said.

"You are mean," she told him as she assumed the position again. He smacked her again, and she squealed. There was still plenty of padding, but those jeans were a lot more protection than her sweatpants, two shorts and five pair of panties.

"You have no idea," he said, and began spanking her. "You think you are cute, don't you?"

"Yes, sir!" she said and gave him a few obliging wiggles. She could feel the spanks, but still.

His voice broke through her smugness.

"Stand up and lose the sweatpants now," he said. "I sure hope we make this reservation."

"We can go now," she said, scrambling up. "I'll take one for the team and forgo the rest of the very painful but very instructive and worthwhile lesson." She pulled her sweatpants off, careful not to lose either pair of her shorts. She was down to what, seven layers now? Surely he'd get tired before she peeled them all off one at a time.

"Get that butt where it belongs," he told her. She took a couple steps away from him, and he grabbed her arm. "Excuse me, young lady. Where are you going?"

"Taking my butt to my computer chair where it belongs," she said.

"Cute." He yanked her back over and smacked her hard enough to make her squeal for real.

"Max!"

He continued the round of smacks as he asked, "How many layers do you have on?"

"Ow! I have no idea what you are talking about! Max!"

"Stand up and peel off the shorts," he said.

Ugh. They were getting down there now. "But I like them, they are comfortable," she whined as she pulled them off and before he could ask or make her peel off another layer, threw herself back across his lap.

"I don't know what I'm going to do with you," he said. "Spank you silly and kiss you properly, I guess."

"Don't forget my surprise later," she reminded him. "Ouch! That hurt! Max! Ow!" Her bottom was starting to sting now. "Ow! I've learned! No more!"

"You will think ouch by the time I get you peeled down to your bare red butt," he said, standing her up. Her knees were beginning to shake a little. Either because of all the scrambling up and down she was doing or the adrenaline from the spanking. "Take the next layer off."

Suddenly she regretted knowing there were five more layers after this one when she kicked off the second pair of shorts.

"Ass up," he told her and she settled back into her now regular position.

Whimpering, she said, "Max, it hurts."

"Spankings hurt," he said, "and you were the one who apparently wanted a really long one."

"Did not! Ow!"

"Did too!" He smacked her about four or five times and she realized her five pair of panties did very little to protect her. But still. Better than no pair of panties.

"Please! That hurt!" She wiggled, trying to move her bottom out of his way.

"And think of how many more you are going to get!" he said. "I'm thinking about twenty for each layer from here on out. How about you?"

"Ow! No, too much and too hard and Ow!"

"Peel another one off," he said, leaving it up to her to crawl off his lap, and look at him.

"Max," she whined and could see him, once again, trying not to smile. Ugh. She wanted to, well, she wasn't sure what, but something!

"Off with them."

Twenty more for each layer? She wasn't stupid, and grabbed two pair, and pulled them both down in one movement, then threw herself back over as a living sacrifice to the spanking god.

"You think you were cute, huh?" he said as he smacked one sore cheek than the other. "Soon as I'm done with this round of twenty, you can put them both back on and we can start over."

"Noo!" she dragged the word out till her twenty were up. Her bottom was getting tingly and warm and she could only imagine how it was going to feel when he was done, with the hundreds of thousands of more brutal smacks he intended to give her.

Sniffling, she stood up and rubbed her bottom. "Max, can't we just cut to the chase and get it over with? Please, pretty please with lots and lots of sugar? I've been good!"

He grinned at her and pointed to the pile of clothes on the floor. "You call that being good?"

"Yes! I thought it was quite clever and innovative and—"

He interrupted her. "Just drop them all and get your bare butt back over my lap so we can finish this up properly."

Why did she feel relief knowing it was almost over? She hastily pulled down the remaining three pair and threw herself back over his lap before he changed his mind. "Not hard! I'm naked under there!" she said. "Ow! That hurt!" Apparently he had no intention of listening to her. He had flipped her t-shirt up and for some reason, she felt mortified he could see her bare bottom and clamped her legs together tightly. He'd seen her naked! They'd even showered together! But still.

"That is one pink bottom," he told her and she buried her face in the couch cushion. "Just begging to be a nice red bottom." He smacked her low and hard and she jerked.

"It didn't say that!" she informed him.

"How would you know? It's right here in front of me and all the way behind you. Now let's make it happy." And with that he started spanking while she jerked and threw her hand back to block him and basically acted like a spoiled brat getting a well-earned punishment, she realized.

Tough crap. No way was she making it easy on him. Bare hurt a lot worse than even a little protection.

Finally it was over and she was curled up on his lap, not really crying, but not really not crying either. Had that been fun? Was it supposed to be? "That hurt," she said.

"It was quite the good time." He agreed with her. "And we both got what we wanted. I wanted you half naked on my lap with some really good bottom heat, and you wanted a nice warm butt while you are in the ice-skating rink."

"Ice skating?" She popped up and looked at him. "I can't ice skate."

"Our lesson is at five," he said. "We have time to get you into something decent, maybe something with some decent padding for your butt you'll be falling on," he teased, " and then we will head over there. I'll walk the dogs while you put some clothes on. Unless you want to skate in that t-shirt and nothing else?" He looked hopeful and she almost giggled despite her sore bottom, that he caused and created.

"I do not," she said and climbed off his lap, for hopefully the last time today.

"Two pair of socks," he suggested as she headed into the bedroom.

"Yes, sir!" Ice skating lesson! With a hot bottom to help keep her warm. The man's thinking process was either really romantic or really weird.

Chapter 5

Lucy opened Moriah's note with trepidation, barely able to believe she had been able to sneak her a note after last week.

I'm okay, just wanted you to know. Mom doesn't know for sure that I saw you but is suspicious, and of course I was punished as if I had. Plus I now have a seven-year-old chaperone with me at all times. She slipped away to the bathroom, so I'm slipping you this note before she gets back. Nothing has changed but my mind set. I might be ready to leave next year. Will wait till after the holidays. I don't want to ruin them for the kids and we both know Mom will do that if I leave. Am saving my pennies and hoping we can somehow manage to talk in the next few months. Gotta go, Love you, Moriah.

Lucy shut her laptop, waves of guilt washing over her. One, she shouldn't be using it on work time. Two, she'd been sneaking into the library to see her sister for a couple months now and obviously they had become complacent. Just as she was leaving last week, her sister Lily had come out of the story hour room early and spotted her. With a big cry of "Lucy" she had made a bee line for her, and it had broken her heart as she had to turn and head out the door, leaving Moriah to block and distract the child.

She'd worried all week about getting them in trouble. Poor Moriah. Though if she was ready to leave, that was a good thing, she hoped. Even if it was a few months away, just the mindset was good. She wished she could get them all out of there, but one sibling at a time, she told herself. Too bad her older sisters and brother wouldn't help, but they were raising their kids basically the same way they were raised. Nothing she could do about it if they were happy. But she could help the ones who weren't. She hoped.

"Hello," she looked up from her desk as her office door opened. "Joni! Jordyn! Why are you here?"

"Ellie called and said to bring lunch. When the big shot city manager calls you, well, you bring lunch," Jordyn said, as she and Joni held up bags and boxes.

"Lucky for us, it's lunch time," Lucy said, and buzzed Ellie. "Lunch is here for you, ma'am," she said into the intercom.

"For us," Ellie called back. "Come on, I'm starving!"

Lucy got up and they all trekked into Ellie's office. Joni looked at Lucy and said, "Man, you are slumming in your office compared to this, huh?"

"Tell me about it," Lucy said. "But then I don't have to entertain royalty like some people."

"She means me," Jordyn told Joni. "I'm the one who brings the decent food. That makes me Queen."

"Darn right," Lucy agreed as Ellie laughed but squirmed a little in her chair. She'd done that squirm before. Hmmm... however, the food smelled good and she needed half an hour with her friends. Her friends didn't know everything, no one would, but they knew of and about some of her past and about Moriah and she needed to talk to them.

"Moriah is finally thinking of leaving," Lucy told them a

few minutes later after they had served each other pasta and a lovely crudité. Jordyn made even sliced veggies look upscale.

"Oh, good," Ellie said. "I know she's been thinking about it. Soon? How can we help?"

Lucy shook her head. "Not soon, not till the first of the year. She doesn't want to ruin the holidays for the kids which, you know, I apparently did after I left. The parental units didn't react well." Understatement.

"It isn't your fault," Joni said, and Lucy looked at her. Of the four of them, Joni knew the least of her past. "Henry told me some things one night after we worked with you at the charity ball. Honestly, Lucy, I thought you were an airhead. I had no idea... well..."

Lucy laughed and cocked her head in her airhead way. "I know, right? I kinda encourage that response in people. Keeps people away from me and doesn't let them, well, get close."

"Lucy has walls," Ellie said, straight faced. "Or maybe she's an onion. You know, with layers." She took a bite of her pasta.

"Ha ha," Lucy said. "Anyway, I have a spare bedroom, but Moriah has no skills, not even a GED. She's almost twenty and would be starting out like a high school dropout. It's going to be a long haul for her."

"Oh!" Jordyn said. "Can she cook?"

Lucy nodded. "Cook and sew and change a diaper. It's all we are good for you know."

"She could intern with me," Jordyn said. "You know I'm working on adding a little catering service onto my business, but I really need some help. I've got my regular clients and enough special parties and things to get me through the holidays, but after that, I want to settle down and focus more on the special things and not do the private meals so much. Give me a little more flex time, let me have a little more fun with food."

"That would be great!" Lucy said. "It would give her a little income while she studied and got caught up."

"Yes, a little," Jordyn said. "But if she is living with you and eating with me, then she shouldn't need a lot."

"And I could get some really yummy food occasionally," Lucy teased.

"I'm a teacher," Joni volunteered, "as you know, and I'd be glad to help her on study skills, navigating getting a tutor through the community college, and getting her a decent career counselor when she's ready."

Lucy's eyes teared up. "You guys are the best. I hope this works out for her. There is nothing wrong with getting married and having kids, but really, there are so many other things in life too. I feel awful that if she doesn't get out soon, that is what she will be doing and then be stuck doing only that for the rest of her life and never knowing what else is out there." She looked around at her three friends. A city manager and aspiring politician, a teacher and a chef. In the next ten years, they would probably all be married with kids, but that wouldn't be all they would ever be allowed to do. She wanted options for her sister. For all her siblings, in fact. Options and education were both very good things and she couldn't figure out why her parents didn't realize that.

There were so many things, despite her college education that she didn't know and had never done. Max had shown her so many in the past month. There was a big, huge world out there and while being barefoot and pregnant was one thing, there were a hundred million more options, too. All she wanted for her siblings was the ability to make an educated choice. Why didn't her parents want that for them?

"Heidi is hosting her annual 'before school' barbeque at the end of the month," Ellie said. "You all need to get with her and find out what she has you bringing." They all nodded. Lucy knew Heidi. Her annual barbeque was legend and huge.

It started late morning and went well into the night, and ended with the kids playing with sparklers and the adults worn out and ready to welcome fall.

She had been going since she was sixteen and Heidi had hosted it for the first time. Ellie's grandma had taken her and Ellie, and Lucy remembered being so mortified at the swim suit Ellie had loaned her. She still didn't know how to swim. She refused to wear such a skimpy outfit in public, but again, couldn't bring herself to put on the ugly modest leggings and long skirts that her parents had let them wade in. Proper girls had no need to swim. They sat on the side of the pool, kicked their feet and watched their little siblings in the shallow end while their brothers dove off the board and had fun.

Rebelling hadn't occurred to her till she entered puberty. Then it hit hard and was the only thing she thought of. Shuddering at the thought of the punishments she'd endured for trying to be herself, she put her mind back to the thought of the barbeque and her friends talking about it.

Heidi's husband was a local doctor, they had a big house, a huge pool and backyard, six kids and almost every other year, it seemed, Heidi was pregnant again. The family had four or five dachshunds running around and Heidi, a nurse who worked a couple days a week at the Health Department, seemed to love her life. See, Lucy thought. Options. You could do anything you wanted, but you need to know options to be able to choose the right one for you. Not have a one size fits everyone mentality.

"Back to school," Joni said, sadly, reaching for a piece of cherry cheesecake. "Summer flew by this year. Teachers all start next week. The kids have two more weeks."

"And Heidi is celebrating the kids going back," Ellie said and laughed and waved her drink. "Can't blame her a bit."

"Here, here," Jordyn said and they all clinked their cups.

"It will be time to start planning the Christmas parade

again, soon," Ellie said, eyes sparkling delightedly. "I can't wait!"

"You and Mike going to be Mr. and Mrs. Claus again?" Joni asked.

Ellie shrugged. "Don't know. I might have to ride with the mayor in her car." She sighed dramatically. "It's hard to be in such high demand." She squirmed again, Lucy noted. Interesting.

"I'll call Heidi later on today," Jordyn said. "I'm actually cooking for them Sunday. They are baptizing the baby and I'm catering the family dinner. I think there are forty of them."

"That is some family!" Joni said.

Jordyn nodded. "But if you all want, I'll ask what she wants you to bring and text you."

"That sounds great," Lucy said. "Thanks." She cocked her head. "My phone is ringing, back to work for me!" She left to go back to her office and a few minutes later waved to Jordyn and Joni as they left while still trying to handle an irate citizen who didn't get their garbage picked up. As if there weren't fifteen other layers to go through before they called the city office. But she had found out her first day, that was part of her job. Her favorite part was talking to them, till they demanded to talk to her boss and then coming back as her boss after a three-minute hold time. No one had ever figured it out, and she soothed her conscience by reminding herself that Ellie kept telling her they were not boss and employee, but partners who worked in a different way, like Mike and Max did.

Hanging up her phone, she started back to Ellie's office to give her the notes and shut the door that had been left open between their offices, when she overheard Ellie talking. "Mike, I swear. I can hardly sit down today." There was a pause and the grand and glorious city manager whined a little petulantly, "No. I don't want another spanking tonight. That was more than plenty. I'm not whining, but my bottom hurts. Fine. I'll stop complaining but it is so hard to sit today and I just wanted you to know it is all your fault! If my friends realized..." Another pause. "I love you too. I still want a seat pillow for Christmas. I'll see you tonight. Yes, I will be home before seven. Yes, I promise. Bye."

Lucy went back to her chair, shaking her head. So Mike was a spanker, too. She wasn't too surprised, because she'd suspected, but it was nothing she was going to talk to Ellie about. Some things were private, even between best friends. Somehow, though, it made her feel a little better about the relationship between her and Max. She wasn't just a crazy kinky weirdo. Semi-normal was more than she expected from life and she was going to take it! Quietly and privately. And most of all, dignified-ly. Just like she took her spankings. Yes. Yes, she did.

Lucy sighed. Fine. He was courting her. But didn't he miss sleeping with her, at least a little bit? Other than kissing, hugging and spanking her, he hadn't touched her in what seemed like forever! She really loved the romancing. She had never felt more... well, cherished? Was that the word she was looking for?

He texted her during the day just to say something nice. He brought her flowers every single week. He took her to dinner. They'd learned to ice skate together, make pasta via YouTube, together they learned to row a boat, plant an herb garden and Jordyn had come over one day and taught them knife skills. They'd gone on many long walks while talking, and even had a dog trainer come over to teach Gypsy and Juliet a couple of cute tricks. That had been hysterically funny. A twelve-year-old yorkie and an eight-month-old shy chi, and the trainer trying her hardest. She had laughed so hard her side hurt. Max could be too much fun.

Of course, that was kind of offset by the fact he found he needed to turn her over his knee and spank her at least twice a week. Sometimes it was fun and she giggled through most of it, and other times she ended up sobbing and then dancing trying to rub out the burn. Either way, for some reason, it brought them closer.

Yet, she wanted to be closer than closer.

Why was she thinking of this on her drive home tonight? Because she wanted Max and he was busy this weekend?

She'd had a challenging day. She and Ellie – well, mostly Ellie and the lawyer they hired – though, she'd been there as back up and moral support, had turned over the accounting report and all the paperwork she could generate to the city board, the town's accounting firm, and another copy to the mayor. The skimming had been widespread and it had cost the taxpayers hundreds of thousands over the last decade. How had no one caught it before? Or if they had, well... Max would have blistered them so hard, they would never sit down, she knew, and imagined that soon, they'd only wished that would happen to them.

Her mind had been boggled at the extent of both the theft and how many people had to be involved. Clearwater could have invested so much more money into the schools, the infrastructure, the park system, helping the homeless and new businesses. So many many things. Ellie had assured her the buck stopped now and with her. This would no longer happen or be tolerated and Lucy felt irrationally happy that Ellie was the public face who would have to handle the fallout from all this, and not her.

Who would have thought something like this could happen in their little town? It just made no sense at all. Sure, she knew there was crime around, there was in most towns, after all. But nothing this serious. It was almost like the college scandal that she'd read about – a bunch of smart, professional people doing something not only really dumb, but really illegal. And why? Money. She didn't feel bad for them. Government workers got paid well, and got benefits most people only dreamed of having. If they needed more, there was always that thing called a second job. She'd worked two jobs a lot, since she was sixteen basically. Even now, she considered her investing a part time job, and did that every day, checking the stock market, moving a bit of money around. But if she had to wait tables or work retail again, she'd sure be doing that too, before she'd steal from hard working people.

She noticed her fingers trembling a little, and thought she needed Max and she needed the comfort Max brought. The security. The feeling that someone would – she stopped and slapped her hand against her mouth. No. She did not need Max to make her feel safe and like an adult. She could do that all by herself. She did do that. Because she was an independent woman.

All they did was play a few little kinky spanking games. She read! People did that! Even if they didn't have the kinky sex that went with the kinky spanking since he'd decided to 'romance' her.

Too bad she didn't drink. How drinking might help, she wasn't sure, but people seemed to lean on it when they got stressed. However, there were no plans for her to lean on either drinking or Max. Lucy knew she was a lot tougher and smarter than she let most people know,

Ellie knew more than most, but Lucy didn't even tell her best friend everything. She had no desire for people to feel sorry for her, and she had no need of anyone's pity. She preferred they think of her as the ditzy little blonde who flitted from job to job and did silly things that they found amusing. That was a good comfortable place for her in the world.

While Max had been slowly leading her away from it, she wasn't certain anymore she wanted to be separated from that person. Ditzy Lucy suited her well, and no one expected anything from her, but an amusing time. Ditzy Lucy had no problems. She was only fun and carefree.

Maybe she should start looking for another job again? Ellie was doing fine and didn't need her to handhold her through this job which was the only reason she agreed to do it. To help her best friend who had helped her so much.

Lucy pulled into her driveway and ran into her house. Why was she feeling overwhelmed? She'd been through worse than handing some papers to a lawyer before. Emancipating herself at sixteen was worse than that. Leaving her siblings at home to endure what she knew they would be enduring was worse than that. Growing up the way she had was worse than that and breaking away from that mindset was even harder. Working two jobs while taking a course load and a half in college had been much worse than that.

All she did today was hand papers over. Even then, technically, Ellie did that. She'd just been there for back up.

Changing clothes, she took Juliet outside and for a short walk, and then went back in, shut and double locked the door and pulled all the curtains, even though it was still light out. Usually she liked to enjoy whatever bit of light there was left in the day. But she felt the need to... to what? Hibernate? Maybe. Luckily, it was Friday and she didn't have to be anywhere until Monday morning. Max was gone visiting his sick dad and had taken Gypsy with him. So he wasn't going to be over. There was all weekend to recover. Recover from what? Paperwork? She did paperwork for a living and she was good at it. She needed to get through the weekend and focus on Monday when she went back to work and didn't have as much time to think.

She'd be fine by then. But for now, she just needed the

comfort of dark and ice cream and Juliet and some mindless HGTV. She could count how many times she guessed which house they picked before they told her, all night long. Her best record was ten of twelve. Lucy settled down on the couch, pillow, blanket, mint chocolate chip ice cream and Juliet by her side, and vowed to beat that record tonight. She'd feel better in the morning.

"Max, Ellie is on the phone. She needs to talk to you," Mike handed him his cell phone. Max stretched out of his office chair where he'd been sending files to Bryan. He'd had a good weekend, even though his little nephew had broken his phone yesterday morning. He would get a new one today during lunch, and the fact his dad was doing much better was a bigger deal than a stupid, broken phone. It had been touch and go, but he pulled through, the doctors were optimistic, there was plenty of family there, and Max felt confident enough in his recovery to come back to work this morning. He'd go back again when his dad was feeling better and some of the extended family went home. Maybe he'd take Lucy with him. His dad would adore Lucy.

He'd driven all night to get here. He and Gypsy hadn't even been home yet. Feeling on a euphoric high because of his dad's health, he didn't care he hadn't shaved or showered. He just wanted to check into the office, give Bryan the files to work on, and then would go home to clean up. "What's she want with me?" Max asked.

Mike just offered him the phone and Max took it. "Ellie? How can I help you?"

"Max? Is Lucy with you?" He could hear the slight edge of panic in her voice.

"No. I haven't talked to her since Friday morning. I've been at my folks' all weekend—"

"And then you broke your phone," Ellie interrupted. "Mike told me. She didn't show up for work this morning and isn't answering her phone. I'm backed up with meetings – really important meetings, Max. I need her here but more importantly, I need to know she is okay. She doesn't miss work and she always answers my calls!"

"Ellie, just be calm, okay? I'm heading to her house right now. I'll call you as soon as I find something out. She probably just overslept or something. More than likely, it's something simple," he said. "Okay, don't worry. Do your meetings. I'll call you or Mike as soon as I can."

"Hang on—" Mike took the phone from him. "Ellie, I'm sending my cell with Max, so if you need me, call me on the office line, okay? Love you. Stay focused on your meetings. Things will be fine. We have this. Talk soon, love you."

Mike handed Max his cell. "Go see what your ditzy girlfriend is up to," he said. "Call me when you find out she's fine and then blister her ass for scaring my wife."

"Will do," Max said, and grabbed Gypsy as he headed out the door. What was going on with Lucy? Mike thought she was a dingbat, but he knew better. That was just a part she played. His Lucy was smart, capable, big hearted and would never frighten her best friend like this. Never. It simply wasn't in her. Something had happened. But what? He felt guilty for not contacting her all weekend. Between the travel, the worry about his dad and all the relatives he'd not seen in forever, the weekend had slipped away from him. That was no excuse for not contacting Lucy though. He honestly had needed the weekend to think about what he wanted with her. Coming to a conclusion had made him feel better but now, because he didn't contact her all weekend, he felt guilty. Surely, like he told Ellie, she was fine and this was just a misunderstanding. Lucy was fine. What could have happened to her? This was Clearwater. Nothing bad happened in Clearwater.

Maybe she just had a dentist appointment or something and thought she'd told Ellie or she might have told Ellie and Ellie forgot. He calmed down. That could easily happen. Lucy would probably be in the office before he got to her house. He hoped so, anyway.

He pulled into her driveway and frowned. All her curtains were closed. She never closed them till dark. Even when she was gone all day, she wanted to walk into light and bright when she got home. He knew that.

He couldn't tell if her car was in the garage, unless he got into the house, and he was getting into the house. There was no doubt about that. He strode to her door, holding Gypsy, and tried the door knob. Locked. Well, that was good. He put the little dog down, and walked to the side yard. Oh, the garage window. He had forgotten about it. Peering in, he saw her car wasn't in there, but he walked around to the back door and tried it, the little yorkie following along. That one was locked, but he knew where she hid her key. They'd hidden it together so he would always know, and she wouldn't have to leave him a note. At some point, he'd like a key, but not until she was ready. However right now, even though her car was gone, he needed to be in this house.

Once inside, he smelled something and heard yipping from the laundry room. Opening the door, he saw Juliet and the evidence of soiled potty pads. That was not like Lucy. Walking into her bedroom, he noticed the bed was made and her phone was on the charger. Great. What was she doing?

Going back into the laundry room, he picked up the soiled pads, put down clean ones, settled Gypsy in with Juliet, then took the soiled ones out to the dumpster, promising them a walk in a few minutes. Okay, he was

MEGAN MCCOY

worrying now. Slamming the lid to her trash dumpster closed, he looked up as he heard an engine down the quiet street.

A wave of relief hit him so hard, his knees almost buckled. There she was. That was her car. His Lucy was safe.

He stood in the driveway and waited for her to pull in. There was someone in the car with her. Lucy looked startled to see him and then started crying as the garage door was going up and she pulled in. What was going on?

He strode to her car and opened the door. She got out and all but jumped into his arms. Max felt her shaking and looked over to the other person in the car as Lucy started sobbing. "Max, I got her, I got her," she kept repeating. Okay. He had no clue what was going on. Got who? From where?

"Lucy," he said firmly and took hold of her arms. "Tell me what's going on."

The other person, taller than Lucy but bearing a strong resemblance, got out of the car and said, "My name is Moriah and Lucy just saved me from a fate worse than death."

Well, this should be a good story, now, shouldn't it.

"In the house," he told her, and held Lucy by her arm as he walked them both inside. "Hello, Moriah. I'm Max."

"I know who you are," she said. "Thank you for taking care of my sister."

Max had no clue what was going on. He led them both to the kitchen island and said, "Sit. I'm making hot chocolate, you are both having some and then I want answers." Lucy was barely holding herself together while Moriah seemed almost icy cold. He wasn't sure which was worse, but called Ellie while the milk was heating up. He got her voicemail. "Ellie, I've got her. She's safe but something is going on. I'll call you again later."

He mixed up two cups of hot chocolate and put them in front of the two women, both of them seemed to be in shock in their own way, he could tell. "Drink," he said in his firmest tone. They needed some strength and he was here for that.

Lucy picked up her mug with two trembling hands and he saw Moriah's were stone cold and steady.

He let them take a few sips and then leaned back against the counter and said, "So. What is going on? Who wants to go first?"

Moriah looked at him and said, "Our parents kicked me out because they found out I was seeing a guy."

"Is he a bad guy?" Max said. "How old are you?"

"He isn't a bad guy, but—"

Lucy interrupted, "Moriah is nineteen and she's not allowed to date. We don't date."

"Well, apparently 'we' do if she got kicked out for doing it," he said. Okay, so a teenager was going against the parents' wishes and got kicked out. It happened he knew.

Moriah nodded. "Yes. I could apparently marry this guy they picked out for me, instead of the guy I wanted to see, or I could leave home. I grabbed a couple things, walked six miles to town—"

"In the dark, in the middle of the night!" Lucy interrupted again.

Moriah nodded. "I finally found an open gas station and called the police."

The police? He kept his mouth shut, hoping the story would keep coming out.

"I didn't have Lucy's number or address, and I couldn't think of anyone else to call. They looked her up and—"

"And sent a cop to bang on my door at midnight!" Lucy was pretty wound up to keep interrupting so much.

"Drink your hot chocolate," he told her.

"So anyway, the cops went to her house, this house," Moriah looked around the room, and halfway smiled, "and Lucy came to get me."

"What time is it? I need to go to work!" Lucy said, sounding utterly panicked.

"You aren't going anywhere, and didn't I tell you to drink?" He affected his stern tone and noticed both of them obediently picked up their mugs. Well, cops at midnight could explain a lot of Lucy's nerves. That would scare anybody.

"So they seriously kicked you out without anything in the middle of the night?" he asked. If you were protective enough not to allow your daughter to date, then kicking her out with nothing in the middle of the night seemed dramatic.

"You don't know our parents," Lucy said. "When I left, they doubled down on the rules for the kids, and who knows what they will do now. But Moriah is here with me now."

Moriah nodded and yawned. "Yeah, here I am in all my glory. No clothes, no job, no high school diploma, nothing but my good looks and charm."

Max half smiled. This one would be fine. That was a teenager's bravado and while he still didn't know what all was going on, she seemed to be a little more practical than Lucy either was or pretended to be. He still wasn't clear on that one.

"I have friends. We are going to get that all straightened out," Lucy said. "At least here you are safe from being forced into a marriage you don't want."

Max didn't know how that could happen in this day and age, but that would be something to find out another day. Right now, though, they both needed a shower and to go to bed and he needed to call Mike and tell him he wouldn't be back today. He knew they would both sleep better if he was here. There would be time to fill in all the holes and pieces in the next few days.

He realized that between his decisions this weekend and what happened this morning, his life had just changed. He was invested.

Chapter 6

Lucy held Max's hand as they walked to Heidi's back yard. She could hear the sound of many children laughing and splashing in the pool and the smell of barbeque. Moriah had gone there earlier with Jordyn to help set up the fancy cake Jordyn had made for the party. Lucy had been in charge of a fruit salad and Max had baked beans. "One pan without hot dogs and one with hot dogs," he told her. "Because that's how I like them."

"And you are the one who counts." She had leaned against him. It was okay to lean against him and lean on him. He had proven himself the first week Moriah had been there, making sure she was safe and settled. Making sure he didn't neglect her was also marvelous. She, too, felt safe and cared for and supported. He was a good and decent man, and how often did you find one of those? Romantic and funny, caring and understanding, strong, yet gentle. Well, except when she was over his knee. Then he was just mean. She'd told him that and made him laugh. But nothing had changed. The price of being with him was having a warm or hot bottom regularly. It was a price she was willing to pay, obviously.

They had both been to Heidi's party before, but not together and looking back, she wondered how she'd missed him? He was hard to miss. But maybe her radar hadn't been pinging to dating yet. Now, it only pinged to him.

The last weeks could have been horrific, but with him in the picture to help her stay calm and focused, they simply weren't. They had simply been changes. A different way of looking at the world. Odd things happening she never thought would.

One of the biggest changes was Mayor Lydia was thinking of resigning because of the money scandal. Even though she hadn't been involved, she felt she should have known. Plus, she said, she was 72 and had no desire to go to court for months during the trial, or to see the people she'd worked with for years in that situation. Ellie had been talked to about stepping in as interim mayor if that happened.

Ellie had asked her, if Lydia stepped down and she did become interim mayor, would she consider being interim city manager. Lucy had rolled her eyes. Those things would probably never happen. Lucy knew she was very happy with her behind the scenes work. She didn't want to go on TV or make public speeches or have many meetings with VIPs. Nope. But they would see how the next few months shook out. She could find another job tomorrow. There was no doubt in her mind about that. So, whatever happened, would.

They put the baked beans down on the hot table and the fruit salad on the cold table. Who owned hot and cold tables? Doctor's families, apparently.

"Oh, there's the dessert table," Lucy said. "Let's go see how Moriah is doing."

They walked through the crowded backyard, and made their way, stopping several times to say hi to people they knew. She saw Ellie and Mike in a corner by the pool, arranging chairs around an umbrellaed table and made a plan to head over that way after she checked on Moriah to make sure she was okay with the crowd and everything. She'd had a lot of changes in the last few weeks. It wouldn't surprise her if Moriah was a little overwhelmed. Lucy knew she had been, for a long time after she had left home. It worried her that Moriah was as afraid as she had been, but didn't feel she could share. It scared her, too, that Moriah had been dating someone she refused to discuss. The reason she'd gotten kicked out of the house in the middle of the night. It was as if he never existed. Or she was still seeing him but afraid to tell her. It would take her a while to feel safe enough to share. Lucy understood that. Her ability to share was still compromised and she often stopped before she did for fear of the consequences. Most of it was ingrained fear, not real fear. She knew that and was working through it. Moriah, so far, wasn't amiable to the idea of therapy. Hopefully, very soon. It would help.

"Hi, Jordyn," she said as she saw her friend arranging cupcakes on a platter. "That is an amazing cake!"

"It is going to taste good, too," Jordyn smiled at her. "Just you wait."

"I will be good and wait," Lucy sighed dramatically, looking down as a small red dachshund rushed through her legs. Cute. Not Gypsy or Juliet cute, but adorable in a sausage kind of way. "Where is my sister?"

Jordyn laughed in a way that made Lucy a little nervous. "Umm, well, she kind of got hijacked."

"What does that mean?" Max asked. Lucy smiled. He'd taken a very brotherly interest in her little sister and she liked that.

Jordyn didn't say anything else, but pointed to the pool. Lucy took a step back and gasped. "No," she said.

"Afraid so," Jordyn laughed. "Heidi recruited her to help watch the kids."

Lucy stared at her tall, blonde sister who had never worn

pants till last week, up on the diving board in a bikini. Her first instinct was to go grab her and cover her up. This could not be happening. What would their folks think? "Max! We have to get her!" she said, softly. "Now!"

He looked at her puzzled. "Get her for what? Jordyn, do you need help?"

"Nope, I'm just putting the mosquito netting over the food and I'm done. Then I'm off to the table with Ellie and Mike to have a couple beers and take it easy on my day off."

Lucy felt as if she were in a horror show as she watched Moriah hold her nose and jump off the board into a crowd of cheering kids. Did she even know how to swim?

"Lucy, what's the matter?" Max asked as he led her away from the crowd. "Are you okay?"

Was she? She didn't know. She was thrilled Moriah was fitting into the 'normal' world so quickly. Shocked and surprised though, was how she felt, she decided. She had never worn anything like that and she'd left when she was sixteen. Plus they'd never been allowed to swim. It wasn't modest! How had Moriah learned? Maybe things had changed a lot more than she thought after she left, and not for the worse like she'd been led to believe.

"Lucy?" Max led her over to the side of the yard. "What's wrong?"

What could she say? That her sister swam and wore a swim suit? That was nothing to get upset about. It was just surprising, that was all. "I didn't think Moriah could swim," she said. "I was scared for a minute."

"Obviously, she can," he said, shading his eyes to look in the pool. "She must have learned."

"Overprotective sister," Lucy said, then took a deep breath and smiled at him. "And I need a huge glass of sweet iced tea."

"Coming right up," he said, and they walked over to

where Ellie, Mike and Jordyn sat. "I'm getting Lucy a drink. Anyone else want anything?"

In reply, they all held up their beer, and he laughed as he pulled a seat out for Lucy and walked away.

"Lucy, your sister is so much fun. She learns so quickly and retains information a lot faster than I did at her age," Jordyn said. "But I'm afraid Heidi is going to steal her from me."

"You think so? Steal her for what?" Lucy asked. When was the last time she and Moriah had sat down and had a talk? It had been several days, she had to admit. Between everything going on at work, and Max taking up some of her time and Moriah working late with Jordyn, they didn't get much time together. Sure, they checked in together every day, and Lucy knew she was around by the mess in the bathroom, but nothing deep and serious had been discussed. That was her fault. She was the big sister and needed to push. Moriah might need to talk. She was probably confused and scared and needed a strong, guiding hand. Lucy felt more than a little guilty about letting her sister down. She'd been through a lot, after all.

"Heidi is looking for a live-in nanny for a few months. Apparently Dr. Paul has a symposium or something or other and will be in Europe for a while. She wants a live-in nanny to help out with the kids while he is gone, and maybe after. Didn't Moriah tell you?"

Lucy shook her head. "No! But we've been like ships in the night this week." Why did that feel like a confession? She should be paying more attention to her sister. She just should. The guilt piled higher.

"Well, Moriah has been spending time here every day since I introduced them at Heidi's friend's birthday dinner I catered, and I think Heidi and Paul are going to offer her the job. But I'm sure Moriah will tell you all about it after she gets the offer."

Well, that was fast. Reaching up, she took the icy glass from Max's hand. "Thank you," she said. She needed to get over herself. Just because it took her years to shake her upbringing, didn't mean Moriah would be the same way. She'd left because she wanted more, an education, freedom, and the ability to make her own choices. If Moriah wanted to go back to her comfort zone of watching kids, well, that was her choice. Not the choice she'd make, but a choice, just like that bikini was a choice. And what a choice it had been.

The fact Moriah had been sneaking out of their parents' house to date some guy she had never mentioned again, oddly, meant their paths would differ greatly. Frowning, she wondered if Moriah knew about birth control. Another thing to discuss. She needed to realize Moriah was not her. That was going to be more challenging than she had thought. For some reason, she really thought that Moriah would want the same things she did. Education. Options. Maybe she just wanted out from under the rules? Maybe she had helped her escape only so she could be wild? Was that a choice too? Was it a viable one and should she be directing her to another path? Lucy didn't know. This was why she didn't want to be a parent. Too many decisions and too many ways to screw up a kid.

She sipped her tea and half listened to the conversation flowing around her while she thought and worried and felt bad about how she'd neglected her sister the last week or so. Once again, looking over at the diving board and seeing her jumping in again, she realized Moriah did not look like she felt neglected.

"Come on, Lucy," Ellie said. "Me and you and Jordyn and Joni are playing lawn darts."

"We are?" Lucy stood up and pulled on her airhead persona like a second skin. "I'm so up for throwing darts at people!"

"Not at them!" Joni cried out, while everyone laughed.

Lucy grabbed Joni's hand and said, "You can be on my side. That way you will probably be safe."

"I'm not sure that is how this works," Joni said, but smiled back at her. "Come on."

"You doing okay?" Ellie asked her as they walked toward the lawn dart game.

"I'm not sure," Lucy admitted. "I'm a little confused about Moriah, a little concerned about work next week, and weirdly, wondering what is up with Max?"

"Moriah will find her way," Ellie said. "She has lots of back up and honestly, staying with Heidi for a while could be great for her. Heidi believes in public school, in getting all her kids a good education and making sure they are ready to be adults. Those are things Moriah needs to understand, that life isn't all about getting married, unless you realize you have other options and that is what you want."

"That is what I want for her. It is just hard," Lucy said. "Ellie, she wore a bikini!"

"And looked darn good in it, didn't she?"

"How would I know?" Lucy asked. All she could see was forbidden skin. Just like she'd felt when she and Mike first got together and to her shock found out he had no desire for pajamas or even lingerie in bed. It had felt extraordinarily naughty. "But I guess she did." She looked like she fit in with the other kids she was hanging out with, anyway.

"As to the office, nothing is going to happen soon on the paperwork we turned in. The law is a very slow, very methodical machine. It could be two years before anything happens, other than gossip when people find out."

"Two years? Really?" Somehow she'd thought things would happen quickly, but then, other than her emancipation which took a month, she had never been involved in a court case.

"Really. Now, the you and Max thing, well, he's nuts about you. But that is something you two will have to work out." Ellie nudged her. "And that is something that will be easier to work out when Moriah moves in with Heidi."

"Is that a done deal?" Why did she feel like she was the last to know? She was not a very good mother figure to her sister, apparently.

"Talk to your sister," Ellie said. "I call blue!" She announced as they arrived at the game site.

Later that evening, Lucy sat with a plate of food on her lap, listening to her friends laughing and talking. She poked at her baked beans, potato salad, corn on the cob and a very yummy pasta dish she needed to find out who made and get the recipe for. She'd not seen her sister all afternoon, but for glimpses here and there. She'd been busy with groups of little kids, and also at other times, with teenagers, seeming to fit right in with both groups easily, as if she'd been with what they had called the 'worldly people' in a not very nice way, all her life. Maybe she was faking it, like Lucy knew she sometimes did when she felt as if she wasn't fitting in. That was where her airhead persona came from. She realized, though, that the longer she was 'out in the world' and the more comfortable she felt, the less airhead she felt she had to act. That was a good thing, right?

Lucy fought down envy as she heard Moriah laugh from across the pool, as she walked back to the table and Max after the game. It had taken her years to feel as if she fit in, but as she looked around the crowded table at her friends, she knew she did. She had a home and a family of her own choosing. All she could hope for was Moriah would find the same.

Finally, as she came back from the bathroom a little later, she ran across Heidi and waved her down. "Thank you so much for doing this every year. It's one of my highlights," she'd told her.

"I love doing it," Heidi said, shifting the baby under her shirt. "It's the best part of the year, knowing the kids are going back to school!" She laughed. "That sounds horrible, but I love my kids and they really love school, most of the time. I only mean it in the best way. The party is a great way to celebrate summer and start the new school year off right."

Lucy smiled. "I was homeschooled till college," she confessed. "I only heard bad things about public schools."

Heidi leaned over and said, "And we only heard bad things about homeschooled kids. Funny how that works, huh? When we are all doing the best we can, I think. But anyway, I think Moriah is going to fit in great, and I plan to help her get her GED while she's here."

Wow. "So it has already been decided?" she asked. "I didn't realize it was for sure."

"Oh, I'm sorry. You just got her back, didn't you? You okay with her moving in here? I can make sure she gets a few nights a week to come back and see you. That's no problem."

Shaking her head, Lucy said, lightly, "Oh, I'm sure it will work out. She does seem to fit in here pretty well."

"I really think she will," Heidi said. "The kids love her and the first thing to do is get her a driver's license so she can eventually help with errands and hauling the kids to school and things. We all just adore her."

Lucy nodded. Sounded like Heidi was going to be a great surrogate mom to her sister. Like Ellie's grandma had been to her. Moriah needed that.

"You ready to go?" Max asked her a few hours later.

"Does Heidi need help clearing up?" Lucy asked as they started to leave. "I don't mind helping."

"You are a little late," he said. "All we have to do is pick up the dishes we brought. Everyone else will do the same and the teenagers cleaned up the other things."

Was Moriah one of those teenagers? Lucy wondered, but

just picked up her empty fruit salad bowl and followed Max out. Moriah was spending the night with Jordyn tonight, because they were doing a lunch for a group of veterans tomorrow. Apparently Jordyn and Heidi had worked out a plan to share her. That was good. She'd be learning some skills, getting some good references, getting a driver's license and her GED. It was really mind boggling if you thought about it. This time last month, she'd been in church three times a week, being a sister mom, trying to study, wearing long skirts and under her parents' thumbs. Now she was a bikini wearing woman with two jobs. How was her head not spinning? The resilience of youth or was she just tamping down her feelings?

"So, what is going on?" Max asked her after they were in the car. "You were very quiet all day."

"Was not," she said, almost automatically.

"Maybe you were," he teased. Then threw her a glance that made her squirm. "So? Speak to me now or later with a sore bottom."

"I need to process," she said. "I'm not dodging, but can I just think a little and talk when we get home?"

"Yes," he said. "You can absolutely do that. I'm not going anywhere tonight."

Despite her mental angst, she hoped that meant what she thought it meant. She really needed him tonight. Needed him to be close to her, to be with her. In her bed. Under her covers. Holding her close. It didn't seem like a lot to ask.

"Let's go by my house and grab Gypsy and then head to yours. You can relax and then talk when you are ready," he said as if it were a non-option and she relaxed. Max was here. He understood.

"You don't understand," she said, later that evening as she sat snuggled on her bright blue couch. "You can't understand."

"Then explain it to me," he said, and she could tell he was trying very hard to be patient.

"Don't you think I would if I could?" He wasn't the only one losing patience. Lucy took a deep breath and put her brain to work. This was a problem to solve, not a drama to be involved in. *Use your logic* she told herself.

"Okay – my upbringing was unusual."

"Clearly," he said.

"Don't interrupt me." She glared at him. "I need to get this out." He saluted and sat back. She assumed that meant okay. Wouldn't it have been easier to say okay?

"Some you know, and most you don't and the most you don't is a story over a few years. I can't deal with telling you all that right now." He gave her an okay sign that made her smile.

"Well, anyway, Moriah isn't acting right."

"Not acting like you would, you mean?" he asked very gently.

"Yes! Exactly. Why isn't she?" She looked at him and saw he was confused. "You don't know." She sat back and sighed.

"Lucy, baby, I can't know. Just like you can't know why she is acting like she is, and she can't know how you think, and how your older siblings justify raising their kids in the same way you tell me they were all miserable. It is hard to get in someone else's brain."

He paused and pulled her close. She inhaled deeply. He smelled so good. "People are different, Luce. You can both go through the same things and react to them differently, understand them differently. Look at me and Mike. We took the same classes in college, we do the same thing, in the same office, yet we both do it totally differently. Am I right? Is he wrong? Or are we both playing to our strengths? Think of Moriah playing to her strengths. This is how she feels comfortable right now. You feel differently now, then you did in college."

He pulled her closer. "Think about it, two years ago, would you have thought you'd be an unmarried non-virgin?"

Lucy shook her head. Nope. That was one thing that had never occurred to her she would be. She always thought she'd be married, legally and spiritually, before she did the deed.

"Yet it happened and while I know you feel some guilt about it now and then, are you sorry?"

She shook her head again and tried to get closer to him. Not experiencing what they had together? No. It had been amazing. Maybe one day he'd want it again? She hoped so. She missed it. It was almost cruel to give her a taste and then take it away.

"I'm scared for her," Lucy whispered. "So, so scared and so worried for the other ones."

"Lucy, you are the only one you can take care of. You can do your best with Moriah, and we will do our best if any of your siblings need help, but…"

"But you have no clue how many I have. You'd be scared if you did." She managed to smile at him. "Max, I'm sorry."

"For what?" he asked.

Did he really not know? She ran her hand against his arm and down to his tight abs. The man was so hot. Not that she really knew hot, but she knew what she liked.

"I kind of need and want you, please? However you want me? I just need you to be close to me and if you tell me no, I'm moving to Las Vegas and becoming a stripper because I'll never be able to show my face in town again." She buried her face in his chest while he stroked her hair and she froze.

That was a 'it isn't you, it's me' move. She knew that one. She read, a lot.

"Lucy, honey, you don't have enough rhythm to be a stripper. I've danced with you. I'm sorry."

"Excuse me?" She was a good dancer! What was wrong with him?

"And I promised myself something," he said as if he almost hurt.

"What? That I'm not worth being with? That I have too many problems and you want to go to someone less complicated like Miranda?" She held her breath. Going to be a stripper in Vegas was low on her list of things she wanted to do, but well, really? Did she have a choice now? How did you even get to Vegas from here?

"No. That I wouldn't sleep with you again till we were married," he said. "I know now that is important to you."

"Is not," she said, head spinning. *Is too,* she told herself.

But she needed, wanted, craved him tonight.

"Lucy, little girls who lie get their bottoms warmed," he said, and pulled her up even closer than she had been. "Do you need a good bottom warming?" He flipped her over his knee and swatted her a few times. Then pulled her up. "I can go full on ass beating if that is what you need."

She might need that, but she wasn't telling him so. That would just be dumb and if she was anything, dumb was not on the list. "I need, I need, I don't know what I need," she sniffled out. "I just am scared of the future, I don't know what is going to happen and I just wanted you in my bed tonight. Like a normal person! It is normal to want some comfort sometimes! And you said no, and I know what that means, and now I'm even more confused!"

She was smart, she knew people needed people. Physical comfort was not a bad thing to want. It did not make her a bad person – just like Moriah wearing a bikini did not make her a bad person. It was going to take a while, and maybe more therapy, to get through the next few years with her sister and her new life, she guessed.

Max hugged her, then got up and strode into her small kitchen while she watched. He reached up on top of her cabinet and picked something up. Had he stashed something up there? Obviously, she told herself. What?

He came back to the couch, but didn't sit beside her. Instead he knelt in front of her and she started crying. No. Just no.

"Lucy, we both have issues. The best way to solve those issues is as a team. Together, me and you. We will have a whole wonderful life ahead, learning our way in the world. I'll give you a family. You will teach me patience, love and caring for even the smallest of things. You and I together, we will learn to compromise and to build a life we will love and can be proud of. Will you, my Lucy, marry me?"

Tears streamed down her cheeks. Barely able to speak, she said, "Only if you stay with me tonight."

"I will never leave you again," he promised. "See, I'm compromising already."

That worked for her. He was a pushover.

Mostly. He had a challenge ahead of him. She smiled as he slipped the ring on her finger. Hopefully, he was up for everything. She sobbed in his arms for a few minutes, feeling happiness, relief and she wasn't sure what else.

After a while, he smacked her bottom a couple times, making her squeak, then reached over and handed her the phone. "Want to call Ellie?" he asked.

How did he know? She grabbed the phone and made her first call as an engaged woman.

Engaged, soon to be married. Only because it was her choice and her decision. Not because she had to be, or it was expected. Because, despite her many other options, she chose to do it, and decided to say yes. And she felt very pleased with both those things right now. And him. And he was staying the night.

"I love you, Max" she said before hitting the button on the phone.

"I've loved you since you hauled that stupid tree into the office," he said.

"I'm going to do stupider things," she warned.

"I hope so. I need a reason to paddle that adorable butt."

"Jerk." She glared at him then squealed "Ellie! Who wants to be my maid of honor!"

Epilogue

Lucy Sutherland drove down the road toward her friend Jordyn's new shop. She'd heard about it via the friend grapevine, and since she couldn't pick up Gypsy and Juliet for another hour, decided to see where Jordyn would be setting up her new bakery. It was a great perk for the square and she hoped this would be a trend that continued till all the empty storefronts were inhabited by thriving businesses. That was her job creeping into her thinking, Lucy laughed to herself. And she hadn't even been there for two weeks while she got married and then honeymooned with the most wonderful husband in the whole entire world. She thought Romancing Max had been amazing, well, Husband Max was double or triple amazing.

Looking around Clearwater as she drove, she smiled. It looked different through a married woman's eyes. Brighter, sunnier, happier, better. Maybe she was just on a honeymoon high still? Who knew that was a thing? Apparently it was, though. They'd gotten back last night and spent the night at her – their – house where they were going to live till Max sold his condo. Then they would decide if Lucy's house suited them or if they wanted to buy another one, a brand new one that neither of them 'owned' but was theirs.

She'd dropped Max off at the realtor's office to sign the papers for his condo listing, and was going to see Jordyn, just a few blocks away, then go get their babies and then go pick him up. Max promised her that on their next honeymoon, or vacation, they could take the girls with them, but he'd wanted her all to himself on this one.

Sighing happily, but squirming a little on her almost welted bottom, she had to concede he'd been right. It had been amazing having him all to herself for a week. Even if he took full advantage of taking full advantage of her. She had loved it. But man, last night, for some reason he decided she needed to be reminded of who wore the pants in the family. He'd found a paddle at some gift store, and made her drop her pants and basically paddled her till she was almost hoarse from crying. Half an hour later, though, she had been happily cuddled in his arms and never wanted to leave. He'd never left bruises and welts on her before but told her it wouldn't be the last. Once again, her weirdness showed up because, for some reason, that made her really happy. Not that she enjoyed it at the time, but, well, the after was more than kind of great.

But now, she felt ready to get to real life, get their dogs home, go back to work day after tomorrow and of course, go see Jordyn's new shop.

She pulled into a spot in the front of the empty shell of a building and hoped Jordyn had decent plans for it. Right now, it just looked sad and neglected. However, she got out of her car and went up to the door, knocked and entered when she saw Jordyn wave her in.

"Lucy! You are home! How was the honeymoon?" Jordyn came over to give her a hug. "Do you love being a married woman?"

"I do love it, who would have thought!" Lucy said. "And

the honeymoon was great. We had the best time. We went to Chicago and went to Brookfield Zoo and The Museum of Science and Industry, shopped on the Loop, took the L, and went to a Cubs game. I'd never been to a major league game before," Lucy confessed. "It was a lot of fun!"

"Major league games are the best," Jordyn agreed. "But the hot dog prices are out of this world!"

"I think you are paying for the ambiance," Lucy said.

"Probably so," Jordyn agreed. "I'm so glad you are back! What do you think?" She waved her arm around the blank room. The inside was painted white brick. It looked white. And like painted brick. The floors were some sort of strangely patterned linoleum that was peeling and stained. However, there was a huge front window, that looked to the east and would be wonderful on sunny winter mornings. She could almost picture a display case of freshly baked pastries luring people into the store.

"Well, it has a lot of potential," Lucy said. It didn't look like much right now. "So what are you going to do with it? Do you have plans?"

Jordyn looked so pained that Lucy instantly knew. "You hired Miranda, didn't you?"

"Not yet, but she's on her way over."

Lucy giggled. "Well, the upside is she will do a great job. The downside is, well, she's Miranda."

"I know, right?" Jordyn moaned. "I have to have this done right the first time. I've been saving to do this for the past five years, and with the bit of inheritance my Grandma gave me, well, it is time. This is the perfect location. I have four rooms but no idea what to do with them. I have a general idea of what I want my kitchen to look like, but don't know the legal details and the, the…" she struggled for the word.

"The legal code? Like everything needs to be up to code?" Lucy asked.

Jordyn nodded and moved her hair from her face. Usually Jordyn had her mass of dark hair in a long braid down her back, but she must have given her hair the day off from rubber bands. "Yes and the rules for the kitchen and the bathroom and smoke detectors and sprinklers and even the flooring, apparently! Miranda knows all that. I just don't want to either get a fine or redo it all in a year."

"I understand, but well, Miranda." Lucy smiled again. "On the upside, Ellie hired her and she dated Ellie's husband. They seemed to do okay. She did great at the new gift shop out at the zoo, and have you been to the Running Water yet? That place is amazing!"

"Yeah, just what I want to hear, another food place is amazing," Jordyn said.

"Sorry," Lucy said, then asked, "have you heard anything about Moriah this week?"

Jordyn nodded. "Yeah, she's taking her GED test tomorrow so Heidi has had her on lock down to study. Then she plans to take a couple classes out at the community college."

Lucy sighed happily. That was what she wanted for her sister. Unfortunately, Moriah didn't want much to do with her and she wasn't sure why, but hoped it was a phase that would pass. She knew Heidi and Jordyn both kept an eye on her though, which was good, though it did make her feel a little guilty. Moriah was her sister, after all! She was the one Moriah had called when the folks kicked her out! Well, as she was slowly finding out, Moriah wasn't her and family wasn't always blood. As long as her sister knew she would be there if needed, then everything would work out.

"So show me around real quick before I have to go, and before Miranda gets here," Lucy said. "What are your plans?"

"I have four rooms and a bathroom," Jordyn said. "This one, obviously will be the show room and where people pick stuff up. I'd like a few little tables or booths where people can sit with coffee and a donut up by the window. Then, over here, is a smaller room. I don't want to do kids' birthday parties or anything, but I'm open to bridal showers or baby showers or something sedate like that. Ladies' lunches or birthday teas. You know."

Lucy nodded. "I could so see that. I can't wait to see what this room becomes!" It could be an adorable little luncheon spot.

"Then there is the little bathroom, but I know it needs remodeled."

Lucy shut the door as quickly as she opened it. "At the very least," she agreed.

"Here is where I want the kitchen." They walked into a huge open room.

"Jordyn, this is going to be so amazing!" Lucy looked around. It was big and empty but she knew Miranda's work and it would be fantastic when it was done.

"Back behind this is a little room, I want to turn it into half walk-in freezer, half office and half pantry," Jordyn said.

"Not that I majored in math or anything, but I'm not sure that works out." Lucy giggled at her.

"Hey, that isn't my issue, now is it? I'm not the amazing designer person, am I?"

"You are not. You are the amazing baker and food cooker person," Lucy said. "We all can't be all things."

"Don't I know it," Jordyn agreed. "Is there any more news on Mayor Lydia?"

Lucy shook her head. "All I know is Ellie called me and said she had a stroke. I haven't heard any updates but will call Ellie tonight and find out. I hope she's okay." She did, for more reasons than just that okay was a good way for someone to be.

They walked back into the big front room. "I just love this

place, I love the windows overlooking the square especially. Everything is so bright in here," she told Jordyn. "I can't tell you how happy I am for you."

"Thank you. I'm working on a name. My grandma's name was Rose, but I worry that people will think that I'm a flower shop if I name it after her. I'm sure I'll come up with one, that isn't too bakery, like The Sweet Shop or too non identifying like Rose's Place," Jordyn said. "You are smart. If you get a brainstorm, let me know, okay?"

"Oh, the pressure!" Lucy fanned herself, then looked out the big front window. "Jordyn, look! It's Paul Bunyon!"

Jordyn joined her at the window, and they gawked at the huge man walking down the sidewalk across the street. "I thought Mike was tall," Jordyn said.

"I know, this guy is tall and big," Lucy said. "He looks like a lumberjack, doesn't he? I've not seen him before, have you?"

"Nope, but Lucy, it looks like he's coming here!"

"No, I'm sure he's just walking across the street, though really he should have gone to the corner and crossed safely," Lucy said.

"Rule follower," Jordyn teased. "But Lucy, no. He is coming here!"

"Maybe he's an inspector or something?" Lucy guessed.

"I guess we are going to find out," Jordyn said. "Hello, can I help you?" she asked as he walked in the door and looked around.

He was huge, Lucy noted. Six three or four, and big. Not fat but he was muscled. Broad and strong, his shirt went to three quarter length sleeves and Lucy noted some tattoos on at least one arm and took a step back. She'd always been told tattoos meant a very rough crowd. She felt in her pocket for her phone in case she had to call for help. He had long, dark hair, a beard, and what seemed to be gentle green eyes. You could never tell though. Sometimes eyes lied. His blue jeans looked worn and his boots had seen much better days. She looked over and Jordyn looked frozen. Was she afraid? Lucy couldn't tell but so far he'd not made a move.

"Hello," he said, and his voice was surprisingly low and gentle. "I'm Ben Collins." He stopped as if he expected that to mean something. Nope. Not to her, but she looked over at Jordyn, who seemed transfixed still.

Okay, she was the grown-up married lady here, she could do this. "Hello, Ben, I'm Lucy and this is Jordyn. How can we help you?"

"I'm supposed to meet Miranda George here," he said. "I guess she didn't tell you."

"I guess she didn't," Jordyn spoke up and Lucy felt surprised. She thought Ben had made her nervous. "But she should be here soon. Why are you meeting her here?"

"I'm a contractor. Miranda wanted me to come over and help her work up some estimates," he said, looking around the room. Oh, okay. He was a worker guy. She looked over at Jordyn and felt dumbfounded. She had never seen her friend look like that before. What was it?

"Miranda should be here soon," Jordyn said and Lucy felt proud of her, but wasn't sure why. "Want me to show you around while we wait?"

"Sure, I'd like that," he said. "Wait. I left my tablet in my truck. I'll be right back."

He left and Lucy looked at Jordyn who stared out after him. "Wipe the drool off your face," she told her. "No. He could be Miranda's boyfriend or have a wife and six kids at home! Stop it!"

"Stop what?" Jordyn asked, running her fingers through her hair. "Did you see the muscles on him?"

"Jordyn, I'm serious! You look like you got hit by a love stick!"

"What's a love stick?" Jordyn asked as if she really didn't care, and Lucy sighed.

"I have to leave to go get my dogs in just a few minutes," she said. "But I'm not leaving you here alone with him."

"Why? Do you think he will ravish me?" Jordyn turned and smiled at her and Lucy felt a little better. At least she seemed to be less transfixed.

"In your dreams," Lucy teased. "Oh! Look! Here comes your designer. I'm going to have to go in just a minute, but I'll wait till she gets in here so I can make a dignified goodbye. I don't want her thinking I'm running from her." She looked at her friend, and said, "You are going to have such a good time fixing this place up. And you get to work with Miranda! Could you be any luckier?"

"Shut up and thank you," Jordyn said. The man, Ben caught up with Miranda and they both watched them walking. "Do you think they are a thing?"

Lucy looked at her and then watched them as they both jaywalked across the street together. The tall, elegant, blonde designer in her high-end clothes, and the lumberjack in jeans and boots. Their body language did seem awfully familiar. Lucy could not imagine Miranda dating at all, but if she did, it would be someone in a suit. In an expensive suit. With dress shoes and not boots. No. Surely they weren't dating? She just couldn't see it. But she'd been mistaken before, of course.

Jordyn walked over to the door and opened it. "Miranda, come on in."

Miranda walked in with her ever-present tablet, and Lucy saw Ben had one now, too. Miranda looked around the room and said, "Hello, Lucy, haven't seen you in such a long time! How are you?"

Lucy tried to keep sweet and tried to put out of her mind the many times Miranda randomly showed up when she and Max were out on dates. Coincidence. Every Single Time. She assured herself. What else could it be? Max had assured her they had never dated.

Smiling, she said, "I'm doing well. I hope you and Jordyn have a wonderful meeting. I have to go, however. Ben, so nice to meet you."

"Oh, I didn't realize you knew my brother," Miranda said. "He just moved to town and he's started to work for me as my general contractor. I just couldn't find good help here in town."

Miranda's brother. Okay, this one was for Jordyn and her utterly besotted look, then. "Oh, that is so wonderful, Ben. New citizens are always welcome in Clearwater. Did your wife and family move with you?"

"Ben is single," Miranda interrupted. "And I only have an hour here, so I hope you don't mind if we get to work?"

"I'll see myself out," Lucy said, grinning at Jordyn mouthing you are welcome, then said. "Call me later, okay?"

"I will," Jordyn said and on her way out, Lucy whispered, "Good luck!" at her.

Then she headed out the door, to get in her car, pick up her dogs and start her new life. Somehow she thought this might just be a new chapter in Jordyn's life too.

The End

See what happens in Jordyn's life – is Ben the gentle giant he appears to be?

Coming soon: The Wife he Needed. Book three in A Clearwater Romance series.

Megan McCoy

Megan McCoy lives in the heartland of America, surrounded by corn, soybean fields and hot guys on tractors. At home, she's raising kids, Chinese Cresteds and poodles, training them all with a tender hand and heart, while saving her sternness for the alpha males in her books. Getting up at three in the morning to write leaves her time for a few hobbies - gardening, canning, bike riding, bread baking and taking in strays.

Don't miss these exciting books by Megan McCoy and Blushing Books!

Clearwater Romance series
The Wife He Wanted
The Wife He Adored

Hometown Love series
Don't Mess with Jess
Hannah and Hawk
Totally Tori
Kelly's Haven
Hometown Love Collection

Her Choice series
His Firecracker
The Dilemma
The City Girl

Her Choice, Always
Her Choice Forever

South Dakota Dreams series
Stormy's Trouble
Talia's Time
Wynter's Waif
Wynter's Wife
Sailor's Search
South Dakota Dreams Collection

Along Came Jones Series
Sebastian
Hank
Logan and Ronnie
Logan's Contract
Along Came Jones Collection

Single Titles
Two Weeks of Joy
An Old-Fashioned Relationship
Hard Wired Desires
Quinn's Comeuppance

Anthologies
12 Naughty Days of Christmas 2016
12 Naughty Days of Christmas 2017
12 Naughty Days of Christmas 2020

Audio-Books
An Old-Fashioned Relationship

Connect with Megan McCoy
www.meganmccoy.com

Blushing Books

Blushing Books is the oldest eBook publisher on the web. We've been running websites that publish steamy romance and erotica since 1999, and we have been selling eBooks since 2003. We have free and promotional offerings that change weekly, so please do visit us at http://www.blushingbooks.com/free.

Blushing Books Newsletter

Please join the Blushing Books newsletter
to receive updates & special promotional offers.
You can also join by using your mobile phone:
Just text BLUSHING to 22828.

Every month, one new sign up via text messaging will receive
a $25.00 Amazon gift card, so sign up today!